ROSIE, VOLUME 3: RECKLESS RAPTURES

Fact or fiction? At this distance in time, it is impossible to tell whether Rosie's diaries are a true record of a young Edwardian lady's erotic escapades or whether, in the great tradition of *The Pearl* and *The Oyster*, they are the work of a particularly lively imagination. What can be asserted without any fear of contradiction is that they lay bare the sensual reality that hid beneath the prim and proper surface of that golden Edwardian era. Having shared her most intimate secrets in Volumes 1 and 2 of her uninhibited diaries, the delightful Rosie again invites the reader to 'lie back and enjoy' further details of her amorous activities as she unashamedly reveals all.

ROSIE: HER INTIMATE DIARIES
VOLUME III
RECKLESS RAPTURES

ROSIE D'ARGOSSE

INTRODUCED AND EDITED BY SIMON GALLOWAY

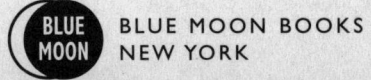

BLUE MOON BOOKS
NEW YORK

Rosie: Her Intimate Diaries Volume III

© 1993 by Glenthorne Historical Research Associates

Published by
Blue Moon Books
An Imprint of Avalon Publishing Group Incorporated
245 West 17th Street, 11th floor
New York, NY 10011-5300

First Blue Moon Books edition 2004
First published in Great Britain in 1993 by New English Library
paperbacks

ISBN 1-56201-431-5

9 8 7 6 5 4 3 2 1

Printed in Canada
Distributed by Publishers Group West

This is for Sheena Walshaw and
Shella de Souza

and moved back a few paces on my knees. 'What are you doing?' she asked with some anxiety, but I assured her that she would enjoy what I had in mind.

'Relax, ma chérie,' I whispered and I bent down and began to titillate the big toe of her right foot with the tip of my tongue. It astonishes me that so few men know that this celebrated Continental recipe for arousing passion is well-nigh infallible, and almost immediately I started this sensuous stimulation, Belinda began to fling herself from side to side, her hands clutching at the eiderdown as she moaned with excitement. Her lovely face was flushed and her body was heaving up and down as I lowered my lips to her ankles and travelled up her legs as she continued to quiver from side to side.

Rapidly moving upwards, I kissed her knees and her inner thighs and when I reached her groin, I buried my face in her crotch, sliding my tongue between the pouting pussey lips which made her scream out with joy. She clamped my head between her thighs as my tongue inserted itself inside the warm, wet crevice of her quim and within seconds her body began to shake and tremble. With a few wild heaves she soon approached her climax and I assisted by licking and lapping around her dripping treasure-trove. I could feel her clitty swell as I slipped my tongue inside her sweet pussey and I probed deeper and deeper until with a few more moans and violent twists and turns she reached her orgasm.

'I want you inside me,' she whispered, releasing my head from its prison between her thighs and she took hold of my shoulders to roll me across on my back. I let myself be so moved and Belinda moved over me brushing her perky pink titties across the tip of my prick which had by now almost fully recovered, and the feel of her rubbery nips over my knob had the desired effect of making my member stand up to a rock-hard stiffness. She grasped my slippery shaft in her fist and rubbed it up and down until I was more than

INTRODUCTION

From the earliest times to the present day, the upper and middle classes in societies all over the world have taken upon themselves the self-imposed duty to protect the lower orders from their own 'base' instincts, and many readers will be aware that when puritanical prudery was at its height during the mid-Victorian era, the sexual act was considered at best a necessary evil and the very idea of ordinary people actually enjoying copulation – even within marriage – was anathema to many worthy citizens.

Indeed, the slightest thought of young, unmarried men and women indulging in the Sins of the Flesh sent shivers of horror down the spines of all but an enlightened minority. As Dr Steve Humphries remarks in his fascinating social history *A Secret World of Sex*: 'the concern with the moral control of young people was of paramount importance and this control was frequently used for religious, political or ideological motives,' though in fairness he adds that there was still much ignorance about contraception, and genuine dangers from several epidemics of venereal diseases at a time when syphilis was incurable and gonorrhea and other sexually transmitted diseases were difficult to treat.

So although some of the suffocating restrictions of the Victorian age may have been eased by the time the *Rosie* novels appeared midway through Edward VII's brief reign, there were still overwhelmingly powerful (if sometimes hypocritical) Establishment voices preaching sexual restraint. One channel of resistance to the smug and often hypocritical doctrines of abstinence was found in the growth of totally uninhibited underground magazines such as *The Pearl*, *The Oyster* and *The Cremorne* which flourished during the 1880s and enjoyed a wide popularity until the outbreak of the First World War.

Many of these were written by journalists working on the fledgling popular newspapers and the *Rosie* novels were written by two young radical feminist scribes, Geraldine Newman and Anna Barnes-Cooney. The first novel, *Her Intimate Diaries*, first appeared in 1907, in twelve monthly instalments of *The Ram*, a spectacularly rude and illicit scandal sheet produced by 'The Friends of Venus and Priapus', a *sub rosa* group of upper-middle-class men and women which held wild parties in London, New York and the South of France. Some four years later, they were published privately in book form by the Scottish racing driver Grahame Johnstone under the false imprimatur of The Edinburgh University Press!

Little is known of this clandestine club except that several characters who appear in Rosie's narrative — the theatrical impresario Richard Tucker; two notorious *roués*, Lord Philip Pelham and Colonel Piers Rankin; and one of King Edward VII's favourite young mistresses, Mrs Sally Cambridge — actually existed and all contributed to *The Ram*, if the recently discovered diaries of the famed Society beauty, Lady Erica Boleyn, are to be believed.

This devil-may-care openness led Professor Barry Barr to comment in his foreword to *Her Intimate Diaries* that the very fact that the authors' friends allowed their names to be used with impunity in the saucy text indicated 'that they believed themselves to be part of a loosely organised, like-minded group and that ordinary members of the general

8

public would always be excluded from this close, private fraternity.

'And it is true that the circulation of this clandestine book was probably so exclusive that the use of real names became a daring indulgence, a kind of curious in-joke amongst the *cognoscenti*.'

This chronicling of sexual adventures in these Edwardian 'horn' books served a useful educational purpose at a time when so many people were racked with unnecessary guilt about their sexuality and even more were lost in total ignorance. However, I am certain that Geraldine Newman and Anna Barnes-Cooney would readily admit that the primary reason for the publication of the *Rosie* novels was financial, for although both girls came from wealthy backgrounds, neither of their families would support their work for Mrs Pankhurst's Women's Social and Political Union, which campaigned for female suffrage or for other radical organisations.

Indeed, when asked by Anna for an increase in her allowance, Lady Marcella Barnes-Cooney not only refused point-blank but added: 'My earnest hope is that the political franchise will not be given to any woman. To give it may be "progress", but in my view it is a progress in the wrong direction. The only possible benefit of admitting women to the franchise might be to show the fallacy of modern democratic doctrines and weaken the belief in purely popular government. As your dear father has often told you, the people will be best served when they realise that government must be conducted solely by the enlightened and the capable − the aristocracy in the strict sense of the word − for the benefit of the masses.'

This drew forth a trenchant reply from Anna, who at the time was in the throes of a passionate affair with Robert Bacon, the handsome young man-about-town, noted sportsman and dilettante of whom Mrs Patrick Campbell

9

once acidly remarked that 'large blue eyes like his might be found in many a stately nursery'.

In *His Mighty Engine*, perhaps the seminal work on turn-of-the-century erotica, the American social historian Dr Alexander Raspie makes the interesting suggestion that Geraldine Newman and Anna Barnes-Cooney based Rosie's adventures in *Reckless Raptures* upon the real-life frolics of Louise Burrell-Jones, the youngest daughter of a brigadier in the Indian Army who for reasons of health was forced to take early retirement and return to London with his family at the turn of the century.

For the record, Louise Burrell-Jones was presented at Court shortly after her eighteenth birthday in September 1902 and she enjoyed an extremely hectic social life with her name often to be seen in guest lists in *The Tatler* but also in more popular periodicals such as *The Harmsworth Magazine* which published her photograph regularly in their *Monthly Gallery of Womanly Beauty* series, a precursor of the modern Page Three pin-up, although all Louise bared was her shoulders!

A few months later, she met King Edward VII in less formal circumstances at one of Lady Bristow's famous country house parties in Worcestershire and by 1905 was rumoured to have been seduced by him at a wild orgy thrown by the King at his house in Biarritz where he stayed every year for at least a month with his favourite mistress, Mrs Alice Keppel. However, a prurient commentator in *The Ram* informs us that His Majesty knew full well that 'his Louise was skilled in the execution of *l'art de faire l'amour*', having already enjoyed several torrid liaisons with the aforementioned Robert Bacon, Lord Philip Pelham (whose raffish sexual appetites were gleefully detailed in *Rosie 2: Young, Wild and Willing*) and one of Edward's famous band of Jewish friends, the merchant banker and noted philanthropist, Sir Ronnie Dunn.

By all contemporary accounts, Louise was a bright and independent girl, and in 1907 she dropped out of the charmed upper-class social circle and joined the small group of radical suffragettes who perpetrated acts of violence (though against property as opposed to people) in their fight to obtain the vote, and in that year went to prison for seven days after refusing to pay a fine for breaking the windows of a jeweller's shop in Bond Street. Like Anna Barnes-Cooney, she was disowned by her family and was forced to live in a small Bloomsbury apartment, although in 1908 her parents paid for her and a friend to spend the summer in Italy, perhaps in an attempt to bring Louise 'back to her senses'. Whether or not this trip had any effect on her is debatable (especially if the narrative of *Reckless Raptures* is based on her Italian adventures) but no doubt to Brigadier Burrell-Jones' great relief, Louise fell in love with Teddy Godfrey, an American architect she met in London, shortly before her twenty-seventh birthday. After their marriage in 1911 she left London for Norfolk, Virginia where she settled happily with her husband and Louise never returned to Europe, although she continued to write to her old friends until the mid 1920s.

Whether she collaborated with Anna Barnes-Cooney in the actual writing of *Reckless Raptures* will never be known, but there is a fresh, robust vitality in the lusty narrative which contains some very frank evocations and descriptions of a wide variety of sexual activity, and there are some stylistic differences to previous *Rosie* novels which suggest that a fresh hand might have produced this particular book.

In any case, whoever the author may have been, it is undeniable that these memoirs clearly show that however repressive the climate of opinion may be, the interest and enjoyment of sexuality will never change, and however much the official culture may try to suppress its importance, there

11

will always be an influential minority opinion which will argue to the contrary and insist that sexuality is one of the most important factors in our lives.

For certain, this jolly romp, published now for the first time in its original unexpurgated form, will amuse and intrigue a new generation of readers of gallant literature.

Simon Galloway
Leeds
July, 1993

I never travel without my diary. One should always have something sensational to read on the train.

Oscar Wilde

CHAPTER ONE

Packing My Bags

I will never forget the beautiful afternoon of the twenty-third of June, nineteen hundred and eight, which I spent in the heart of the Welsh countryside. After a picnic luncheon, Lord Philip Pelham and I climbed to the top of a steep hill and we had looked down at the fresh, deep green of the valley below us, watching the silver stream glisten in the summer sunshine as a warm breeze caressed the backs of our necks.

I turned round to speak to Philip who was standing a few yards away but I tripped over a small mound of earth and stumbled into his arms. He held me and wordlessly pressed the length of his body to me, kissing my lips, my face, my throat and I clung to him as we sank to the ground . . .

But before I continue, I must retrace the events which led me to this beautiful, unspoiled part of the Principality and begin the story five weeks earlier when a letter arrived for me from Susannah Meverson, an old school friend from St Hilda's Academy for Young Ladies, inviting me to spend a long weekend at her parents' country home in the wilds of rural Pembrokeshire.

Susannah had written that in the absence of her parents in France, she was holding a lawn tennis weekend and amongst the guests would be Anthony Wilding, the Cambridge University champion and Gabrielle Renaud, the winner of the French and Italian tournaments and, knowing my enjoyment of the sport, she hoped that I would be able to come to her family's house deep in the Welsh countryside near the little town of Cardigan.

It had been an especially pleasant duty to write back to Susannah and tell her that I would be accepting her kind invitation for, frankly, I had not thought that my parents would allow me to attend this gathering. Besides having to undertake a long journey to South West Wales from the Sussex coast with only a servant to escort me, I would have to stay overnight in London at an hotel, for our town house in St John's Wood was undergoing extensive renovation and would be out of use for another four weeks. Also, when Mama read in Susannah's letter that Lord Philip Pelham was planning to join the party, I assumed she would ensure that I stayed at least a hundred miles from Pembrokeshire for she nursed a shrewd suspicion that, behind her back, Philip and I were carrying on a clandestine love affair. However, when she read that Susannah's aunt, the formidable Mrs Augusta Sheringham who had written several articles in the society papers about the need for strict etiquette to be observed between young people, had consented to act as chaperone [*an older or married woman who supervises young, unmarried girls on social occasions – Editor*], I finally managed to persuade Mama to give her consent to my plea to be allowed to spend a few days at Meverson Hall on the condition that Dennison, our footman, accompanied me there. I had no objection to this arrangement as I needed a strong pair of hands to look after my luggage and his accommodation at Meverson Hall would cause no problem for my hostess as Susannah would expect most of her guests to bring a servant with them.

Of course, readers of my earlier reminiscences [*see 'Rosie 1: Her Intimate Diaries'* and *'Rosie 2: Young, Wild and Willing', New English Library – Editor*] will know that my

Mama's misgivings about Lord Philip Pelham were not without foundation. I must confess that the young scamp had been fucking me for some six months now and the cheeky rascal had even used my name under a lightly disguised pseudonym in his essay for the literary competition for a prize of one hundred guineas offered by *The Oyster* [*perhaps the most spectacularly rude of all the many underground magazines of late Victorian/Edwardian times – Editor*]. Contestants had been asked to compose between fifteen hundred and two thousand words about their most enjoyable sexual escapade in 1907 and Philip had penned a racy account of my eighteenth birthday party when he and I (and later Miss Fiona Brookchester) had threshed around naked in my bed after the other guests had left Argosse Towers for their own homes. But that is another story best left untold, especially now that Miss Brookchester is engaged to be married to Lieutenant Harold Elton-Potts of the Grenadier Guards.

By happy chance, the day before I was due to leave home to begin the long trek to Pembrokeshire, my parents also left the house to go to Edinburgh to attend the wedding of my mother's niece to the Duke of Midlothian. After waving goodbye to Papa and Mama outside our front door, I went back inside to supervise the packing of my luggage for the journey. I was going to entrust the packing of my clothes to my personal maid, Elaine, who was by far the most proficient at this tiresome chore than anyone I have ever met, but Sayers, our old butler who had been in service at Argosse Towers since before I was born, informed me that Elaine was nowhere to be found.

'Very well, Sayers, but ask her to come up to my bedroom when you do see her,' I told him, but I speculated that I would discover Elaine's whereabouts well before the faithful old retainer. I slipped out of the house through the back door and made my way to the motor-house [*the word 'garage' did not come into general use until after World War One — Editor*].

Elaine and I had few secrets [*see 'Rosie 2: Young, Wild and Willing — Editor*] and I knew full well where Elaine disappeared to — and why — during the day. She was conducting a torrid liaison with Jack Dennison, the footman who was to accompany me to Wales, and I rightly guessed that she had taken him out to the motor-house to enjoy a quick spooning session before going upstairs to pack my cases.

As I quietly approached the empty building (my parents were being driven to Euston Station in North London by Haines, our chauffeur, in our new Rolls Royce where they would catch the night sleeper to Edinburgh, and my young brother Jonathan had taken out the Mercedes for a spin with his best friend, Charles, the dashing young son of Colonel Nettleton who lived some two miles down the road towards Midhurst) I could hear faint sounds of panting and sighing which confirmed my conjecture that Elaine and Dennison were engaged in a spot of rumpy-pumpy.

I walked softly towards the door which the randy couple had carelessly left slightly ajar and peeped through the gap, and saw my maid and footman entwined in the most amorous of caresses, both stark naked on an old mattress that Haines used to lie on when inspecting the undercarriage of our motor-cars, upon which they had thrown an old blanket and a couple of pillows, doubtless filched from the housekeeper's cupboards. This was not the first time I had seen Jack Dennison fuck one of our female servants in the motor-house. A few months ago I had come across him coupling with Kathie, a scullery maid who had also entertained my naughty old Uncle Lord MacChesney and, in consequence, had subsequently gained a position as housemaid in his bachelor apartments in Curzon Street, Mayfair.

Elaine was a prettier girl than Kathie, full-bodied though

18

not run to fat, firm and curvaceous everywhere with large, rounded breasts and a smooth white skin which set off to good effect the mass of dark curly hair that nestled at the base of her belly. To be fair, I should also note that Jack was a good-looking young fellow, broad-shouldered and wide-chested and, as they kissed and canoodled together, I saw his hand cup one of Elaine's soft breasts whilst she slid her fingers round the thick shaft which was standing up between his thighs, and Elaine's nipples seemed to grow before my eyes and they appeared to almost stab at Dennison's palm as he fondled each delicious bared breast in turn.

Then suddenly he scrambled to his knees and Elaine lay down with her head on the pillows as he knelt between her parted legs. She then pulled his head down to her bosom and turned his face from side to side, kissing each engorged, stalky tittie in turn whilst his right arm reached down so that his hand was set between her legs and his fingers played inside the silky forest of hair which covered her prominent mound.

My hand stole down to rub my own moistening pussey as I watched them kiss, and I saw Jack Dennison's hand cup one of Elaine's large, bare breasts whilst she grasped his thick, erect shaft which had risen up between his muscular thighs and rubbed his truncheon up and down, capping and uncapping the wide mushroom knob. Her raised-up red nipples seemed to grow before my eyes as they appeared to stab at his palm as he fondled each beautiful bosom in turn and she continued to slide her hand up and down his blue-veined boner.

Then, suddenly, she was forced to release his huge cock as he scrambled to his knees and knelt between her parted legs whilst Elaine lay on her back with her head resting on one pillow as she slid the second under her bottom. Then she pulled his head to her breasts and he turned his lips from side to side, kissing each engorged, rubbery nipple. Now he reached down so that his right hand was between her thighs and I could see his fingers play around inside the silky bush of dark curls which covered her mound.

He parted the pale pink lips of her cunney which protruded through the nest of pubic hair and her body twisted and turned as she rolled her belly on his stiff, throbbing tool whilst he sucked her tingling titties. Elaine threw back her pretty head and moaned with passion as he brought her up to the very peak of unfulfilled desire. However, I was delighted to note that Dennison was a skilled and considerate lover for, instead of simply ramming his rigid rod inside her honeypot, he first ensured that Elaine was ready to receive his pulsating prick.

Quickly, he pressed his fingertips against the open, sodden slit of her cunt, flicking at the erect little clitty that had already peeked out, and only then did he take hold of his huge, erect cock and thrust his helmet between the yielding lips of her juicy cunt, and Elaine gurgled with joy as he propelled inch after inch of hot, pulsing prick inside her love channel until their pubic hairs were matted together.

For a few moments he stayed still with his shaft totally embedded inside her but then he pulled back slowly and drove back down again, pushing his full length inside the gorgeous girl, repeating the movement again and again, faster and faster as she urged him on, closing her feet together at the small of his back to force very last millimetre of cock inside her soaking cunney. She drummed her heels upon the base of his spine as he pistoned his prick in and out of her clinging sheath, but such passion brought matters to a swift conclusion and with a gutteral cry of 'I'm coming, Elaine, I can't stop!', Dennison jerked up and down in a frantic rhythm before withdrawing his glistening, wet cock for one final plunge and he crashed home, spurting his seed inside Elaine's willing womb as he sank down upon her.

'Wow! You must have shot a pint of spunk inside me,' said Elaine as she ruffled his hair with her long fingers. 'But you don't have to worry, I made sure to douche my pussey with a good dollop of linseed oil [*a crude but relatively effective contraceptive used widely at this time, although not as good, of course, as modern birth-control methods – Editor*] before we began. Not that I'm really bothered as I've only just finished my monthlies, but it's better to be safe than sorry, isn't it?'

'I should say,' panted the lucky lad. 'Oh God, that was a wonderful fuck, Elaine, but I'm sure I came too quickly for you. No, don't try to fool me, I know you didn't spend.'

'Don't worry, I still enjoyed myself,' she assured him with a loving kiss. 'And anyhow, we had to finish quickly or Miss Rosie will come looking for me. I should have started to pack her cases at least fifteen minutes ago. Gosh, I wish I were going with you, Jack, you lucky devil. I'll miss you, you know, I really will.

'And I'll miss you too,' she added, bending down to plant a smacking great kiss on his still semi-erect shaft which was dangling over his thigh. 'Promise me that you won't be dipping into any strange pussies whilst you're away.'

Dennison looked down briefly at the tousled head resting in his lap, but then he sighed and he reached across for his clothes. 'Chance would be a fine thing! Look here, much as I'd love to have my cock sucked, we'd better get ourselves dressed pronto and get back to the house, for it would be wrong for you to take any liberties with Miss Rosie, she's a real toff. Why, I bet that if you told her why you were late and that you hurried our love-making, she would have told you not to have been so silly and to have waited till you had spent.'

I smiled at this compliment and left them to dress as I strolled back to my bedroom. Five minutes later Elaine knocked at my door and apologised for her absence. I did not wish to embarrass her but I could not resist saying: 'Are you feeling well, Elaine? I hope you're not letting anything get on top of you?'

'No, Miss Rosie, everything in the garden's lovely, thank you,' she replied pertly as she opened the door of my wardrobe.

Yes, and things aren't too bad in the motor-house either, are they? I thought, but I refrained from mentioning what I had just witnessed and simply showed Elaine which of my clothes I wished to take to Meverson Hall. I had purchased a compressed cane dress trunk from the Army and Navy Stores on my last visit to London. This new case was rather an extravagant purchase, as Papa commented when he wrote a cheque to settle the account, for it cost ninety shillings and sixpence [*£4.52! — Editor*]. But as I pointed out to Papa, it was fitted with a tray for accessories, and had straps all round with a double action lock, very necessary to foil the growing number of sneak thieves on the railways and elsewhere.

This reminded me to make sure that the present for Susannah I had ordered from Mr Selfridge's new store in Oxford Street was securely packed in my best valise, a large Imperial with two lever locks and two keys. I hoped she would like my gift, a Picnic Compact gramophone with a Swiss motor that played two twelve-inch records with just one wind of the handle, and I left Elaine to her work and went downstairs to ensure that the machine had not been taken out of the wooden box in which it had been delivered by Selfridge's carrier.

Looking back with hindsight, I suppose I should have rung for Sayers or Dennison, one of whom would have come up to my room but I needed to write an important letter before leaving for Wales. This was to Antoine Delvoie, a young Swiss gentleman of my own age with whom I had enjoyed a brief if fervent relationship during my stay at a

22

finishing school on the beautiful banks of Lake Lucerne some two years before.

Antoine and I wrote to each other regularly, not only because we wanted to keep up our friendship, but because from the start of the correspondence we agreed to keep up our familiarity of each other's language. Antoine would write in English and I would reply in French! Dear Antoine always gallantly insisted that my French was better than his English. Alas this was not the case, although I possess enough knowledge of the language to read Monsieur Zola or Victor Hugo in the original, a great benefit, for much is lost even in the most sympathetic translation.

Before going to the library to write to Antoine, I decided to seek out Sayers and find out whether Susannah's gramophone had been securely packed as I had instructed — but what a shock I got when I entered the butler's pantry! For there standing stark naked against the wall was the plump figure of Lizzie, the vicar's youngest daughter and old Sayers, who was still in uniform except for his trousers and underpants which were lying over his ankles, was busy slewing his prick in and out of her hairy pussey.

At first I stood unseen as the butler's lean bottom cheeks jerked to and fro as the couple rocked in time as they pursued this amorous exertion. Then Lizzie let out a scream when she saw me looking on at this lewd scene. Sayers spun round and I was surprised to note the prodigious size of his prick which was definitely longer than Dennison's although perhaps not quite so wide in girth.

The old retainer's face went white and he clapped his hand over his mouth, but I was irritated rather than offended, and that only because all the servants seemed to be enjoying a good fuck today whilst it had been a full fortnight since I had enjoyed the sensation of a nice, thick prick inside my pussey, and that only a brief hour snatched with my brother's friend Michael Beecham in his rooms in Great Titchfield Street.

Meanwhile, Lizzie and Sayers stood transfixed until I said: 'Don't mind me, you two, I'll happily wait until you've finished.

'Yes, you mustn't keep a lady waiting, Sayers,' I added, rather enjoying the butler's discomfiture. 'Her need is greater than mine.'

I winked at Lizzie who giggled and said: 'Come on then, Sayers, you heard what Miss Rosie said, let's not waste any more time.' And to encourage him, she turned round with her feet apart and stuck out her rump so that her chubby buttocks were pushed out saucily towards him. Sayers cleared his throat as he shuffled between her legs and nudged her knees apart, taking his sizeable shaft in his hand.

'Are you ready, Miss Lizzie?' he asked and, after receiving a quick nod of assent, he guided his gleaming member into the crevice between her bum cheeks, before sliding through into the warm, welcoming wetness of her cunt.

Then Sayers showed the truth of the old saw about many a good tune being played on an old fiddle, because as soon as his prick was safely ensheathed in Lizzie's cunney, he started to fuck her in a slowish but regular rhythm. He reached round to fiddle with her large, tawny nipples, tweaking them between his fingers as he continued to slide his cock in and out of her sopping slit. Her backside slapped enticingly against his thighs as he increased the pace, and she wiggled her bottom from side to side as she cried out: 'Harder, fuck me harder, you randy old goat!'

He obliged by increasing the pace, withdrawing his tool almost completely before pushing home and sheathing his shaft so fully at each stroke that his balls banged against her bum cheeks.

'I'm coming, oh, I'm coming, yes, yes, YES!' screamed the uninhibited girl and she shuddered to her climax with a screech of pure ecstasy. Seconds later Sayers' torso went rigid and his sturdy old tool expelled its emission of frothy jism into her seething crack. She yelped with glee as the glorious sensations of her own orgasm swept like magic through her body and she twisted her bum lasciviously to draw out the last drains of sperm from Sayers' twitching todger.

'Oh, that was wonderful, let's do it again,' beamed Lizzie brightly, turning round to show us her shining face.

'I'm sorry, but I'm not up to it, Miss Lizzie. Besides, I mustn't neglect my duties,' said the butler as he pulled up his trousers. 'What can I do for you, Miss Rosie?'

I explained my concern about Susannah's gramophone, but he assured me that the machine had been packed in its original case and would come to no harm on the journey to Pembrokeshire.

'Very good, that's all I wanted to know,' I said and turned on my heel and walked away, but Lizzie called me back. 'Rosie, have you a moment to spare?' she asked with a worried expression in her voice.

'Of course I have,' I replied. 'When you're ready, meet me in the library and perhaps Sayers would ask Mrs Moser to prepare a pot of tea for us.'

Ten minutes later we were sipping tea together and, after exchanging some idle trivialities, Lizzie leaned forward and took my hands in hers. 'Rosie, I am so embarrassed being caught *in flagrante delicto* with your butler,' she said, blushing furiously as she added: 'I just don't know what came over me. It isn't that we haven't indulged before. You may as well know that Sayers has been fucking me regularly for the last three months.'

'This is a matter solely between you and him,' I said gently. 'It does not concern me or, come to think of it, anyone else in any way whatsoever, and of course you may completely rely on me to keep my silence about what I saw just before in my butler's pantry.'

'You are as kind as a sister,' said Lizzie, rising up to kiss my cheek, 'and if I can ever repay you, be assured I will never hesitate to do so.'

'Well, thank you, Lizzie, I appreciate what you say,' I replied and the girl looked at me with a mischievous smile. 'Oh, come on, Rosie, surely you're dying to know how I became intimately involved with one of your servants. You certainly have a right to know.'

I returned her smile and said: 'I can't deny that this question did cross my mind, but as I just said, this matter concerns only the two of you.'

'Oh, I don't mind telling you about it,' she said, settling herself into her armchair. 'It all began when I heard a sermon from Mr Kavanagh, Papa's new curate. You've not met him, have you?'

I shook my head, for, like both my parents, my brother and I are firm agnostics and attend Church only for baptisms, weddings and funerals.

'Well, Mr Kavanagh is a Christian socialist and when Papa was unwell one Sunday, he asked Mr Kavanagh to preach and he delivered a rousing address on the iniquities of the present political system,' she went on, leaning forward with her knees pressed tightly together. 'He took as his theme the Sermon on the Mount, and he captured my attention in a way which frankly my father has never managed to do.'

'What did he have to say?' I enquired, for I was curious to know how a young curate could so affect Lizzie.

'Well, pretty much what I have heard him since repeat at political meetings in Midhurst and Crawley,' she said. 'He explained how there has been an unparalleled increase in our powers of production which has resulted in huge accumulations of wealth. But only the owners of capital have benefited, while for the great mass of people there has only been an increase in misery and insecurity. He argued that the working classes will no longer endure this unfair division

26

of society and he contrasted the lazy, luxurious lifestyle of the well-off with the hard labour of factory workers and the humiliating subservience demanded by the wealthy from the vast army of domestic servants.'

'I say, that's a bit strong,' I commented with a frown. 'I wouldn't have thought that our staff believe they are being exploited at Argosse Towers.'

'That's exactly what Sayers said after the service, but after Mr Kavanagh finished his discourse, one of Farmer Searle's labourers muttered loudly: "Well, if Socialism means fair shares of pussey for all working men, then I'm all in favour!". Fortunately, Mr Kavanagh did not hear this *sotto voce* comment and I congratulated him on his sermon. However, I'm afraid that Sayers was not convinced and we engaged in a long discussion as we walked through the village together. I invited Sayers into our home for some refreshment and we continued our argument. My mama and my sisters were visiting her cousin in Pulborough and I had stayed behind to minister to my sick papa who was suffering from a severe feverish chill. I went upstairs and saw that he was sleeping peacefully and then returned to continue my debate with Sayers.

'I opened a bottle of claret and I really couldn't tell you just how it happened, but after a while I found myself sitting on the sofa (for by now we were on first name terms) and my sensual appetite would not be denied.

'He played with my breasts, cupping them in his hands through the thin material of my dress and underslip, and I moved my hand to the front of his trousers and felt the hard stalk that threatened to tear the material which covered it. His thighs moved as he tried in vain to ease his erection, but I had already decided to offer a helping hand. So great was my desire to hold and play with his stiffstander that I unbuttoned his fly and grasped his thick shaft which showed out of his trousers, quivering like an arrow. Nothing

27

loath, Cuthbert unbuttoned the top of my dress and caressed my naked breasts as I rubbed his hot, hard cock up to peak condition.'

Lizzie paused and sipped her tea before continuing: 'When I judged that he was on the point of spending, I took my hand away and we locked ourselves into a lingering, erotic kiss with our tongues probing inside each other's mouths. I kissed him all over until my lips found their way to the purple, uncapped crown and I popped the pulsating knob between my lips, jamming down his foreskin and lashing my tongue around his fleshy staff. I sucked hard, drawing at least half of his extraordinarily long cock into my mouth whilst I toyed with his hairy ballsack. Then I started to lick this lovely lollipop, drawing my wet tongue all the way from his balls right up his shaft and I ended by washing his helmet with saliva and lapping it up with the edge of my tongue which made him moan out loud with pleasure.

'His cock tasted like nectar and I took all of his knob back inside my mouth and eased in the rest of his throbbing tool. I bobbed my head up and down on his shaft and three short licks and one long fierce sucking was enough to send him off. He released a torrent of hot, salty spunk which cascaded down my throat. Cuthbert has quite enormous balls, by the way, and only by swallowing convulsively could I gulp down all of his copious emission. Of course, I was now dying to be fucked, but unfortunately my papa chose this time to wake up and bang down on the ceiling with his stick to demand my attention.

'However, we were not to be denied and we arranged to meet on his next afternoon off, which happily was only two days away, and we consummated our relationship in Farmer Searle's meadow on the banks of the little stream which runs round the south side. And from then on, we have made love regularly, Rosie, and very nice it has been, too. There is much to be said for a more mature lover. Cuthbert might not be able to fuck with the vigour of an eighteen-year-old, but he doesn't shoot off before I'm ready, and he knows a trick or two about lovemaking that comes only with experience.'

'Or by reading my papa's copy of *The Oyster*!' I grinned, and Lizzie burst out laughing. 'More than likely,' she agreed. 'Does your Papa receive *The Oyster* regularly? I've only seen the magazine once, but it was far more interesting to read than *Hymns Ancient and Modern*!'

We finished our tea and I escorted Lizzie to the front door. 'Good-bye, and do come again for a chat,' I said as we shook hands, and then I dropped my voice as I went on: 'My parents are away for a few days and I've been invited down to Wales to spend a long weekend with an old friend. Only my brother Jonathan will be here and he is out most of the day with Charles Nettleton, so I am sure that Sayers will have plenty of time on his hands.'

Her eyes lit up as she heard this welcome information and she gave me a warm hug before turning away and walking briskly down our carriage drive. I chuckled as I sauntered back to the library. Since my sixteenth birthday I have had my own private drawer in the large desk there (the study boasts a beautiful, late-Georgian mahogany desk but, as Government papers are occasionally stored there, the study tends to be out-of-bounds to all except my father). [*On the very first page of her diaries, we are informed that Rosie's father is a senior Civil Servant in the Foreign Office — Editor*]

But first I wanted to read Antoine's last letter to me in detail before I dashed off my reply, for I had only previously scanned through the first couple of pages. He had written about how he had met up again in Paris with one of my contemporaries at the finishing school in Lucerne, a Scottish girl named Belinda Briskin from Inverness. As I took the sheets out of the envelope, I remarked out loud how I would wager a pound to a penny that Antoine spent at least one night in her bed, for Belinda was one of the friskiest fillies at Madame Dupont's establishment.

I was soon proved right as this extract from his letter shows:

So, my dear Rosie, on the second evening of her stay, Belinda managed to slip away from her wealthy aunt and uncle who were accompanying her on the trip to Paris to which they had treated their niece as a present to celebrate her nineteenth birthday. When Sir Ronald and Lady Jennifer Briskin suggested a post-prandial walk down the Champs Elysées, Belinda pleaded a slight headache and retired to her rooms.

I was waiting in the hotel lobby and once I saw Sir Ronald and Lady Jennifer disappear out of the hotel, I sent a message up to Belinda's suite and five minutes later we were sitting on her bed, drinking iced champagne. We chatted about the fine times we enjoyed whilst Belinda was studying at Madame Dupont's and when I mentioned your name, Rosie, saying that I wrote to you regularly, she asked me for your address as she would also like to correspond with you. She also asked me to send you her very best wishes (which I now do) and inform you that she is now residing at Gibson House, Chester Street, Edinburgh should you wish to write to her.

Then, as I remembered how Belinda always enjoyed a good joke, I told her the story of the Englishman who went to a club privé in Berlin and spent the night with one of the girls there. In the morning, he got up whilst the girl was still asleep and dressed himself as he had arranged an early-morning business appointment, so he put a five pound note on the bedside table and shook the girl's shoulder to wake her up.

'What's all this?' said the girl sleepily and he replied: 'Just

a little payment for your services, Fraulein,' but the girl looked at the note and said: 'Mr Smith, I'd rather have marks.' So he coolly put the note back in his wallet and said: 'Very well, my dear, eight out of ten!'

This made Belinda laugh so heartily that she spilt some champagne down her skirt. I took out a handkerchief to help mop up the damp patch, but she was not unduly distressed and said: 'It will dry out soon enough if I hang up the dress now. In fact, why don't we both undress now because I can hardly wait for you to make love to me and I far prefer to fuck naked.'

So, without further ado we stood up and I took off my jacket whilst Belinda threw her dress over her head, an action which revealed that the naughty girl had already dispensed with her underclothes. Her beautiful bare breasts with their jutting pink nipples and the abundant thatch of fluffy blonde hair between her thighs fired me with great desire, and my penis instantly swelled up to an almost painful hardness as I struggled to rid myself of the remainder of my clothes.

Once we were both naked, I covered her mouth with passionate kisses and then, suddenly, Belinda dropped to her knees and her pretty flaxen ringlets were between my legs as she kissed my rampant rod which was standing up as stiffly as a guardsman outside your Buckingham Palace. The tip of her tongue flicked and licked all around the ridge of my unhooded helmet and, when she opened her lips and encircled my knob, instinctively I jerked my hips forward to push my prick further inside her sweet mouth.

Belinda looked up at me with a wicked smile as her tongue washed all over my stiff cock and her teeth scraped the tender flesh as she drew me in between those luscious red lips, sucking in almost all my shaft which sent shivers of delight coursing through my whole body. Now she circled the base of my truncheon with one hand whilst with the other she gently squeezed my balls, and she started to bob her head back and forth, sucking my prick with gusto in the most sensuous of rhythms. Then she let my twitching cock fall from her mouth as she changed her ministrations to down below, nibbling upon the soft, wrinkled skin of my ballsack which sent me into fresh paroxysms of the purest pleasure.

Finally she switched her attentions back to my penis and she palated my prick wonderfully as I plunged my quivering chopper down her willing throat. I let out a great shout and spent copiously, filling her mouth with a hot gush of sticky seed that gushed out of my throbbing cock. She gulped down my ejaculation with great enjoyment, smacking her lips as she swallowed all my spunk, licking and lapping until my sated shaft started to shrink and I lifted her to her feet and led her to the bed where we lay down together on the soft eiderdown.

'Oh dear, I feel so randy, Antoine, though I suppose your poor little dickie needs a little rest,' she sighed, flicking my flaccid shaft with her finger.

'I'm afraid so, but I'm sure I can pleasure you in other ways,' I replied with as much gallantry as I could summon, and I hauled myself up to kneel between her creamy thighs. 'M'mm, are you planning to lick me out?' she enquired eagerly. 'I do hope so, Antoine darling, because the British are so backward when it comes to the noble art of eating pussey that I can't remember the last time I was brought off this way. And I do have a pretty pussey, don't I, darling?'

'It's beautiful,' I said in a low voice and Belinda smiled contentedly as she thrust her hips upward as I dipped my head down and imprinted a kiss on her cute little cunt, pressing my mouth to her cunney lips in a long, clinging embrace.

But I wanted to assist Belinda to climb the highest peaks of erotic delight so, to her surprise, I pulled my head up

32

ready for the fray. Then she squatted over my straining knob and guided it between her squishy cunney lips, and my cock slid all the way up her sopping slit as I reached up with my hands to squeeze her proud young breasts.

Belinda rode me with powerful movements of her supple thighs. I began to move with her and played with her luscious, red-stalked nipples, rubbing them to bullet hardness whilst she rode me at an ever faster pace. Ma foi, *Rosie, this was no slow, lingering fuck — we were both so urgent in our needs that with every thrust downwards upon my prick, I rose up to meet her with equal vigour.*

We enjoyed this superb fuck for as long as I could hold out, but then the tingling in my cock became stronger and I could feel the first gush of sperm forcing its way up inexorably from my bollocks. My prick twitched uncontrollably and I thrust my hips upwards and jetted a fountain of sperm inside Belinda's cunt as her love channel quivered all round my shaft and she started to spend herself in a glorious mutual climax. The muscular contractions of her cunney increased my pleasure even more and I shot a second, tremendous spurt of spunk into her juicy honeypot and she fell forwards into my arms, shaking and yelping in delight as her cunney poured out its own liquid tribute, and the mix of our joint spends dribbled out of her crack and soaked the eiderdown.

We lay exhausted for some minutes, still coupled together, sucking in great gulps of air, and for a while neither of us could speak. Then Belinda smiled at me and puckered up her lips to blow me a tiny kiss. I lifted her gently off my hips and looked sadly down at my now shrunken organ. 'I regret that for some time I shall be hors de combat,*' I remarked sadly, but Belinda gave my prick an encouraging rub and said: 'Your dickie has worked very hard and deserves a rest. Anyhow, I'm not sure that I can carry on for a while. My poor pussey also needs time to recover.'*

Suffice it to say that I spent the rest of the night with Belinda, licking and lapping, fucking and sucking in all sorts of ways. We were not interrupted by her uncle and aunt who thoughtfully decided not to disturb their niece when they returned from their evening walk, and instead played bridge with Colonel Piers Rankin and Mrs Sally Cambridge who also happened to be staying at the same hotel. Is it true what the more salacious French magazines are writing about Mrs Cambridge? They say she is rivalling Mrs Keppel for your King's attentions these days, but then as you English say, one must never believe what one reads in the newspapers.

Write back to me soon, Rosie, and be sure to be as frank as I have been with you. The encounter I described above took place ten days ago and since then, alas, I have lived like a monk. Well, not like some monks who are notorious 'arse-bandits'. Is that not the correct English colloquialism? I have been called many things, but never one of those!

Finally, I must convey best wishes from Mademoiselle Justine de Villeneuve [see 'Rosie 1: Her Intimate Diaries — Editor] *who wishes to be remembered to you.*

All my love,
Antoine

I took a deep breath as I put down Antoine's lovely letter. Truth to tell, his erotic epistle had made me so randy that I needed some instant relief. I rushed upstairs to one of the spare bedrooms and locked the door behind me. I swiftly undressed and stood naked in front of the long wardrobe mirror, letting my gaze run down to the flaxen pubic hairs which curl over my crack, and slowly but surely I rubbed my finger all along my moist slit. Then I reached up and took out a small box which I had prepared for such occasions, in which I had placed a hand mirror and the divine ivory dildo Countess Marussia of Samarkand had kindly sent me from Cairo as a birthday gift a few months before.

Then I placed the mirror on the carpet between my legs and, by crouching down, I had a marvellous view of my love lips which I separated with my fingertips until I could see to the very depths of my now wet, tight cunney. As I closed my eyes and pictured Belinda's lithe, gleaming body rocking up and down upon Antoine's stalwart shaft, I pushed two fingers inside my honeypot to get the juices flowing and sure enough, in no time at all, my pussey was dripping wet.

I picked up the dildo and eased its smooth ivory head between my yielding cunney lips, slowly manoeuvring it round and round, touching my little clitty which spread wonderful waves of sheer ecstasy out from my pussey all over my body as I watched myself in the mirror. Then I rushed over to lie down on the bed and, opening my legs, started to slide the artefact in and out of my cunt, ever faster and deeper until, whoosh! A genuine orgasm shuddered its path through me as my cunt exploded and my love juices flowed unabated. I stayed still for a minute or so and then ambled into the bathroom where I sponged myself dry and washed the dildo with soap and warm water, feeling much rejuvenated by this solo gratification.

Perhaps I should add at this juncture that unlike so many young people, I have never had any qualms about masturbation. On my thirteenth birthday, my dear mama left by my bedside a copy of *Human Procreation Explained for Boys and Girls* by the noted Harley Street specialist, Dr Iain MacGregor. Therefore, unlike so many of my unhappy contemporaries, I have never felt unnecessary guilt about this practice, for although Dr MacGregor assures his young readers that self-stimulation is a quite natural and completely harmless pursuit, several misguided physicians still insist that it can lead to the most fearful illnesses such as blindness and softening of the brain. What absolute bunkum! How can there be any harm in it? Certainly, no boy ever caught an unwanted infection from tossing-off, and no girl ever found herself *enceinte* through finger-fucking.

Be that as it may, whilst I was slipping back into my clothes, my reverie was interrupted by the sound of raised voices from below and I hastily buttoned up my dress and went downstairs to investigate. The commotion was coming from the servants hall and when I arrived there, I was startled to see our cook-housekeeper, Mrs Moser and the village schoolmaster, Mr Whiteman, standing there in their coats which were literally covered with mud and a foul-smelling substance which looked suspiciously like manure. Our usually placid cook was red-faced with anger and was loudly cursing Mr Jerbutt, one of our neighbours, whilst Elaine, Dennison and Sayers were attempting to brush off the dirt from her clothes.

'What's going on here?' I demanded loudly. 'Mrs Moser, what on earth has happened to you? Have you been involved in an accident?'

'No accident, Miss Rosie, because three sacks of horse manure were quite deliberately thrown all over Len and me,' replied our cook hotly.

I looked at her in astonishment. 'Who was responsible for this outrage? We should report the incident immediately to the police.'

The mild-mannered Mr Whiteman coughed and said: 'I'm afraid that wouldn't do much good Miss d'Argosse. You see, the perpetrators were none other than your neighbour Mr Jerbutt and his men, Davies and Muttley.'

'Does that matter? Surely they can be charged with assault,' I remonstrated, but the schoolmaster shook his head and went on: 'Mr Jerbutt is Master of the local hunt and all the local magistrates are members. In any case, the matter would never be brought to court because he is also friendly with the senior officers of the Mid-Sussex police force through his Masonic connections.'

'Nevertheless, I want you to tell me exactly what happened,' I insisted, sitting down on a chair as I waited to hear his story.

He shrugged his shoulders and said: 'Very well, but I still don't think there is anything that can be done.

'Mrs Moser and I were walking back from the school (it was a half-holiday today) and we had planned to spend an hour or so on the Downs finishing off our water colour paintings.'

'Really, I didn't know that you had any artistic leanings, Mrs Moser, although perhaps I should have guessed from the exquisite pictures of the countryside on the walls of the kitchen. Were you responsible for them?'

'She certainly was,' intoned Mr Whiteman. 'As you may know, I hold a painting class on Sunday afternoons and Mrs Moser is without doubt my most talented pupil.'

His words cooled our cook's anger and she said rather coyly: 'Now then, Len, don't embarrass me like that. Take no notice of him, Miss Rosie.'

Mr Whiteman smiled and continued: 'We were walking along the Midhurst Road when one of the hunt followers, whom I recognised as James Davies, rode up and began questioning a young girl in a cart which was standing on the side of the road. After many loud enquiries as to the whereabouts of the hounds and how far he was behind them, he spurred up his horse and galloped past us, bespattering us both with mud from his horse's hooves. I shouted my anger but he spurred up, acknowledging my words with a rude gesture which there is no need for me to repeat in front of you.

'A minute or so later, Mr Jerbutt and Herbert Muttley rode up and brusquely enquired as to whether we had seen Davies. "Yes, and he is responsible for coating us with mud," I said sharply but Mr Jerbutt, whose demeanour and breath plainly showed that he had been drinking heavily, simply laughed out loud, calling out to Muttley: "Haw! Haw! Haw! Look at this pair, they would hardly need any make-up to play in one of those nigger minstrel shows!"

'For sheer boorishness and absolute disregard for people's feelings, I have never seen anything to equal his behaviour. Naturally, Susan, Mrs Moser that is, was very angry at this caddish behaviour and she said as much. But then Muttley peered down at us and said to his master: "Don't worry about these two, sir, I've heard this fellow speak out against hunting in the pub." He may have been referring to a discussion there last week when I quoted the late Oscar Wilde who categorised fox-hunting as "The unspeakable in pursuit of the uneatable".

'Well, they rode off in a swaggering way but as Mrs Moser and I were making our way back here, the three of them came charging back, each holding a sack of manure, dismounted and tipped the contents of their sacks over us before riding off.'

'If my papa were here, he'd make them pay you damages,' I said angrily, looking across at Mrs Moser's new coat which Elaine was doing her best to clean, a tailor-made double-breasted Cheviot serge garment with velvet trimmings and lined to the waist with silk, for which she had paid fifty-seven and sixpence [£2.88! – *Editor*], a huge sum for even a well-paid servant such as our cook.

Elaine looked up and said with a giggle: 'I've just thought of a good idea of how we could get our own back, Miss Rosie, but I think I'd better tell you about it in private.'

I did not question her as to why she should want to speak to me secretly, for Elaine was a bright girl and I trusted her judgement. 'Very well,' I said and motioned for her to join me in the hall.

When we were alone, she looked round to make sure that no-one could hear and said: 'Miss Rosie, you know that I'm friendly with Millie Fosberry who works at Colonel

Nettleton's house. Well, Millie has been carrying on with Mr Jerbutt for the last two or three months. She's a very naughty girl because she doesn't like him all that much but her dad's been out of a job since he broke his leg at work last November, and her mum's doing her best to try and keep the family out of the workhouse.'

'Oh yes, Fosberry was quite a hero, wasn't he? I remember reading about the incident in the local newspaper. Didn't the poor man get injured trying to stop a runaway horse?'

'That's right, Miss Rosie, only as it happened on his way to work, his employer gave him the sack, and even though she's taking in washing, Millie's mum is finding it a struggle with three young children, though Millie gives her as much as she can,' Rosie explained. 'So Millie was tempted when Mr Jerbutt offered her a sovereign [*one pound – Editor*] to come round to his house and be nice to him, as he put it, whilst his wife was away.'

A frown settled on my brow because, although I am a true libertarian when it comes to enjoying a good fuck, I do not approve of married men straying from the straight and narrow, although as will shortly be seen, I was forced to bend my rule in Wales with none other than – well, dear reader, you must wait and see.

Meanwhile, Elaine was about to tell me more about Mr Jerbutt's sexual peccadillos when Sayers came out of the kitchen and said: 'Excuse me interrupting, Miss Rosie, but Mrs Moser wants to know if Coq Au Vin will suit you tonight for she needs to begin work on dinner as soon as possible. Oh, Elaine, your friend Millie Fosberry has come to see you.'

What a happy coincidence! I told Sayers that Coq Au Vin would be lovely and that he should send Millie out to us immediately. 'My goodness, I quite forgot that it's her afternoon off and that she was coming to sit with me this evening,' said Elaine. 'She'll tell you all about Mr Jerbutt herself.'

Millie Fosberry was a slim young girl of no more than eighteen years of age who sported a mane of long, dark hair, large blue eyes and a pretty *retroussé* nose, and I could see why Mr Jerbutt had been attracted to her. At first, Millie was reticent to talk about her experiences with him, but after a little persuasion she confided in me that the first time she had gone round to his house, Mr Jerbutt had been very civil to her and plied her with all kinds of delicacies, and together they had drunk a bottle of the best French champagne.

'Then we went up the stairs to his bedroom,' she confided as we moved into the drawing room and sat down on the sofa. 'And as I knew what I was expected to do for my sovereign, I started to take off my clothes and I heard him groan when I slid my slip down and let him see my bare breasts. He seemed shy so I cupped them in my hands, stroking the nipples till they stood up and I said: "Well, aren't you also going to undress?" and he replied: "That's capital, capital!" and he came forward and squeezed my bum before sitting on the bed and taking off his shoes and socks. But he seemed to hesitate so, to put him at his ease, I tugged down my knickers and stood stark naked in front of him, and then he unbuttoned his shirt and pulled down his trousers and stood up wearing only a pair of white linen drawers.

'I yanked them down and looked down at a mass of wiry black hair from which dangled a thick, well-formed prick. Of course, I just could not understand why that juicy looking cock wasn't already as stiff as a poker, jutting upwards ready and waiting for me! I sank to my knees and kissed the tip and drew back the foreskin to uncover his knob, but I simply couldn't make his cock swell up, despite taking his helmet inside my mouth and licking it all over.

' "Why, Mr Jerbutt, don't you fancy me?" I asked with

a genuine note of reproach in my voice, for although I was only there because I desperately needed the money for my poor family, frankly, I felt rather sorry for him.

'I allowed his soft shaft to fall from my mouth and he said in a strained voice as he pulled me to my feet: "Ah, Millie, there is something you can do to help me to a cockstand if you are willing." I nodded guardedly and silently he bent down and from under the bed he produced a stout black Malacca cane. He led me by the hand to the bed and for a moment I was frightened in case he wanted to beat me with it, but I soon found out that the opposite was the case because he placed the cane in my hand and bent over the bed with his face pressed against a pillow, his legs spread wide and his feet firmly on the floor.

' "Go on, Millie," he said, his voice muffled in the pillow. "Crack away!"

' "Where?" I asked hesitantly.

' "On the arse, you silly girl," he replied sharply. "Give me six of the best and you'll see my cock stand to attention."

'This was all new to me, but I grasped the cane and still with some reluctance brought it smartly down across his dimpled bottom.

' "Harder, Millie, harder!" he called out, waggling his bum cheeks, so I laid on three more strokes, raising long red weals all over the surface of his backside. He wriggled and writhed as the stinging cuts of the cane fell with a swishing sound on his firm white buttocks, striping the skin in all directions, and I felt the beginnings of a warm glow all over my body as I laid on a fifth cut to the deep crease of his arse. He arched his naked rump to me and I struck the final stroke across both cheeks which made him yell out: "Ow! Ow! Ow! That'll do, that'll do!"

'I laid down the cane as I felt this warm glow spread out from my pussey to my breasts and the back of my neck. Mr Jerbutt stood up and faced me and, my goodness, what

42

a difference the beating had made! His cock was now rock hard, standing up as straight as a die against his belly and he drew back his foreskin himself, making the pink knob swell and bound in his hand.

'What a magnificent stiffstander he could muster once he was aroused! I could hardly grasp it in my fist, even though my fingers aren't particularly stubby. But Mr Jerbutt was so urgent to insert his rampant weapon that I simply lay down on the bed and opened my legs and let him enter me. And I must confess that I enjoyed the fuck as he pushed his massive member slowly between my cunney lips until I could feel the full length of his shaft inside my love channel. He pumped away enthusiastically, stroking in, holding himself in place and then slipping out in a quickening rhythm as his balls slapped against the back of my thighs.

' "You fuck like a lady rather than a mere servant," he said breathlessly, a cack-handed compliment but I said: "And how does a lady make love?"

' "Oh, she gives and takes with equal gusto," and I laughed at this, saying: "Then you must fuck me like a gentleman would," as I wrapped my legs around his back. He moved up slightly so that his prick slid in and out at a higher angle and tickled the edge of my clitty. I wriggled my hips wildly as Mr Jerbutt increased the pace and I soon spent and my love juice coated his cock as it ploughed in and out of my well-oiled cunney until he let out a hoarse yell and shot a stream of hot seed into me.'

'Did he give you the sovereign he promised?' I enquired, and Millie nodded. 'Yes, eventually, but I had to wallop his bottom again and then suck his cock before he would give it to me.'

She turned to Elaine and added: 'As it happens, I walked over to tell you that Mr Jerbutt has told me to be at his house at five o'clock if I want to earn another gold coin. So I'll go there now and come back here afterwards if that's convenient.'

'I've an even better idea,' said Elaine excitedly. 'I'll come with you if it's all right with you, Miss Rosie. Don't worry, I'll be back in plenty of time to finish the packing for your trip tomorrow.'

I was puzzled by her words. 'Why on earth do you want to go with Millie to Mr Jerbutt's house?' I asked, and she replied with a sly smile: 'Well, if you would let me take along your brother, Mr Jonathan's, Secret Waistcoat Camera, I would photograph Mr Jerbutt fucking Millie and then we could warn the old bugger that if he didn't pay for a new coat for Mrs Moser and for the cleaning of Mr Whiteman's clothes, we would show the photographs to his wife.'

Now whilst I could appreciate the rough justice in such a scheme, I could not agree to my maid's plan. 'No, I don't think so, Elaine,' I said with some reluctance. 'Because in my experience the end rarely justifies the means and Mrs Jerbutt would be hugely embarrassed even though she is innocent of any wrong-doing.

'However, the scheme is not totally without merit. What you could do is to photograph Mr Jerbutt in a ridiculous rather than a compromising position. Millie, perhaps you could persuade him to wear something silly whilst you are whopping him. Then we could warn him that if he did not make suitable redress, we would release the photographs and he would be a laughing stock around the county. To be honest, I still have grave reservations for, despite our good intentions, the idea is still blackmail by any other name, but at least we would not be greatly hurting Mrs Jerbutt by exposing her husband as an adulterer.'

'Oh yes, Miss Rosie. Why, Mr Jerbutt said he was going to dress up as a schoolboy this afternoon and I should pretend to be his housemaster and cane him for being a naughty boy,' said Millie, her eyes shining with excitement at the thought of Mr Jerbutt being humbled. 'But I don't know how he would feel about letting Elaine watch.'

Elaine smiled at this and said: 'Leave that to me, Millie, you would be surprised how when their pricks are stiff, most men lose any common sense they possess, especially if they believe that they are going to get their cocks sucked!'

I could not help but agree with these sentiments and I said; 'Very true, and so long as you confine yourself to snapping shots of Mr Jerbutt being caned on his bare bottom, then you may have Jonathan's camera and proceed with your plan. I don't think it necessary to inform him unless he returns before you, Elaine, though in the circumstances I'm sure that Jonathan won't mind our borrowing his property without his permission.'

'I know where he keeps it, Miss Rosie, shall I bring it down?' asked Elaine with a wicked grin spreading all over her pretty face.

'Very well, you naughty girl,' I sighed and she rushed off upstairs to fetch the camera, a small circular affair which could be attached to one's clothing and was ideal for sneaking a quick snapshot, for all the wearer had to do was pull a short string that opened the shutter and hey presto, a photograph was taken on the glass plate inside it.

Elaine returned with the apparatus and said with satisfaction: 'There is space for four more photographs on the plate, which will be enough for us.'

'All right, off you go, girls, and good luck,' I said, although I still felt a little doubtful as to whether I was right to give my consent to what was afoot. 'Elaine, please try not to be too late as you still have to finish packing my clothes.'

'I'll be back in good time,' she promised, and the girls scuttled out to keep their assignation whilst I informed Mr Whiteman and the other servants that I had set in hand a plan to compensate them financially, even if an apology from the awful Mr Jerbutt was probably too much to ask.

'In the meantime, give me your measurements and I will

45

write to my tailor, Mr Rabinowitz, who will make you up a nice new summer coat,' I said to Mrs Moser. 'Only last week he sent me some sketches from a French magazine which I'll give to you and you're bound to find something that you'll like in it. There was one design with a tight-fitting back and a pouched front, lined to the waist with silk that I thought would suit you down to the ground. Don't worry about the cost, Mr Jerbutt will cough up, I assure you.'

Mrs Moser thanked me profusely, but she was still a trifle nervous and she said: 'It's very kind of you to trouble yourself, Miss Rosie, but just suppose you're wrong and he doesn't pay up. I can't afford five pounds for one of Mr Rabinowitz's coats.'

I thought about Elaine snapping away with her secret camera and said grimly: 'I am so confident that I will tell him to put the garment on my account if I am proved wrong and Mr Jerbutt does not pay handsomely for his disgraceful behaviour.'

Having sorted out this dispute, I went back to the library to compose my reply to Antoine whilst Elaine and Millie were busying themselves on their righteous mission, for there would be little time in Wales for me to write back to my dear old friend and I knew how much he enjoyed reading my letters, especially when they were nice and spicy! Before I sat down at the desk, I searched for a French dictionary, for remember, dear reader, that I had to reply to Antoine in his own language. I decided to take out the large new Larousse I had purchased at Mr Blow's bookshop in the Charing Cross Road, but to my great surprise, as I pulled it from the shelf, an envelope slipped out from between the pages and landed on the carpet. I picked up the envelope which was addressed personally to Mr Blow. My only excuse for what followed was that the envelope was already open . . .

I took both the book and the envelope back to the desk

and took out the perfumed pages of expensive writing paper. I opened them up and immediately recognised the address printed in raised letters on the first sheet: *Stomson House, Hurstpierpoint, East Sussex.* Only yesterday I had been glancing through the pages of *The Tatler* in which there were photographs taken at the ball given by Lord and Lady Stomson to celebrate the twenty-first birthday of their eldest daughter, Pamela.

Mea culpa, I succumbed to temptation and read the letter which turned out to be not from Lady Stomson or Pamela but Angela, their seventeen-year-old younger daughter. She began her epistle by thanking him for sending her the twelve volumes of the complete Shakespeare she had ordered, and then she commented roundly upon the letter he must have sent her with the books:

You indicate some surprise that Mama queried the price of five pounds plus postage for my books. Well, yes, they may be printed in clear, bold type with numerous illustrations and bound in best, half-polished calf with gilt top edges, but I do not believe that you are in a good position to judge whether this price is expensive. I have always understood that booksellers are deluged with advance gratis copies by publishers' representatives hoping to solicit orders. True, a new book is cheaper than dinner at a good restaurant or a seat at the Opera, but in these fast times, I regret to say than many people would rather enjoy a decent meal at Baum's Chop House [a fashionable establishment in Bloomsbury patronised by the fast young set — Editor] *or patronise the Empire Music Hall, Leicester Square rather than sit for hours and hours wading through a heavy novel by Sir Walter Scott, Charles Dickens or Robert Louis Stevenson. So the book trade cannot afford to sit on its laurels and must offer a wide selection of new, exciting young writers at popular prices.*

Anyhow, talking of books, I had the most extraordinary experience the other day. My young fifteen-year-old cousin Toby was staying with us for the weekend with his parents and on Saturday afternoon, everyone except me went out for a constitutional after luncheon. At least, I thought everyone had gone out when I wandered upstairs to my bedroom where I had left a magazine which I had been reading. However, as I was crossing the landing, I heard a sound like a creaking bedspring coming from Toby's bedroom. The door was closed and normally I would have probably ignored it for one of the maids might have been up there, but recently, according to the local newspapers, there has been a spate of housebreaking around this neighbourhood, and so I put my eye to the keyhole to see if anything was amiss.

My goodness, what a shock I got! For there was Toby lying naked on his bed holding a book in one hand and massaging his stiff, swollen shaft with the other! And this was no boyish little tool that Toby had between his legs but a splendid specimen of a fully grown cock, large and strong, in the full flush of youthful power and beauty. He had drawn down the white skinned cover from his knob which gleamed redly as his hand slicked up and down his proud pole. Oh, but Toby looked so sweet lying there and I gazed upon his slim, lithe torso with wonder and admiration, but naturally it was his erect prick and surprisingly big balls which most attracted my eyes.

A warm glow spread all over my body and as I watched him rub his meaty tool I felt a moistness between my own thighs and, pulling up my dress, I started to finger my cunney through the thin material of my knickers. Indeed, I felt randier and randier until I just could not bear it any longer and, after giving my damp pussey a final fingering, without further ado I opened the door and marched straight in!

Goodness me, Toby's face was a picture! In an instant,

all the colour drained from his cheeks and he dropped the book and released his shaft as he tried somewhat ineffectually to cover his cock and balls with his hands.

'Jesus Christ! What are you doing here, Angela? I thought you were all going out for a walk!' he blurted out wildly. 'Oh God, what shall I do!'

For reply, I said quietly: 'Do? Why, Toby dear, you do not have to do anything at all,' as I closed the door behind me and turned the key in the lock, an elementary precaution which poor Toby had failed to take. 'Now it's nice to play with yourself, but I know an even better game,' I continued smoothly, opening the buttons of my blouse and sliding the garment off my shoulders. He looked on open-mouthed as I continued undressing and giving my young cousin his first view of the naked female form.

I did not bother wasting time in preliminary foreplay but immediately reached for his cock, which was no longer fully erect but still thick with unslaked passion. His shaft sprang back to life in my grasp, swelling up to its previous proud, hard state. For a young lad, it was surprisingly large, for Toby isn't particularly big for his age. Yet believe me, I am not exaggerating when I tell you that his erect prick must have been at least seven inches long and his pubic thatch was quite dense, with the hair lying in a sweeping wave over the base of his cock. However, I then remembered listening outside the door at a dinner party after the ladies had retired and the men were passing the port and dear old Dr Macdougall was telling Papa that Edward confronted Lily Langtry [one of Edward VII's most notorious mistresses when he was Prince of Wales — Editor] *about the fact that her pubic hair was much darker than the hair on her head. According to Dr Macdougall, this is by no means unusual, and many a blonde woman has been wrongfully accused of dyeing her hair after an intimate encounter has revealed a dark pubic bush.*

49

Slowly at first, I ran my fingers up and down the length of Toby's tool and then I tightened my grip and began to slide my fist up and down and then delicately encircled the uncapped, bulbous crown and lowered my head to implant a kiss on it. This excited my poor cousin so much that I only had time to lick his rounded knob once more before his boner began to twitch and he reached his climax with sperm shooting out from his cock and trickling down my fingers. As the sticky white froth came bubbling out of his knob, I jammed my mouth over his helmet and slurped up his jism which I found very pleasant to taste, being less tangy than yours, dare I say, and juicier than that of Lieutenant George Lucas of the Household Cavalry who fucked me last month at Annabel Blumer's coming out party. I gulped down every drop of Toby's copious emission until his tadger shrank back, not to a complete flaccidity, but to a sensuous semi-erectness.

I lay down on the bed and gave Toby the chance to explore my body. 'Oh, Angela,' he said, his voice cracking with emotion. 'You are such a beautiful girl and I've dreamed so often of fucking you whilst I've been wanking. Just looking at your breasts, God, those lovely red titties . . .' and his voice trailed off as I gently pulled him to me and I took his hand and encouraged him to roll my nipple against his fingers until it was as hard as a pebble.

He kissed my neck and throat with great fervour and then moved down to my breasts and sucked hard on my pointy titties whilst he rolled himself over on top of me and brought the crown of his erect-again prick to my waiting pussey lips.

Without hesitation I grabbed his cock and with my own hands guided it to its destination, and the sensation of his throbbing, virgin prick squeezing into my quim made me tingle all over with excitement. A deliciously ecstatic feeling spread all over my body and I went off into a little series of delirious spends which oiled my cunney so nicely that

Toby was able to squeeze every inch of his iron-hard boner inside me, and I revelled in the sensations afforded by his young, meaty cock within the soft, luscious folds of my love sheath.

My cunt was now on fire and as a marvellous climax shuddered through my veins I felt Toby's body go rigid and he shot a glorious flood of jism inside me. His spunk spurted with such intensity that I could imagine it splashing off the rear wall of my cunney and, indeed, so abundant was his spermy ejaculation that my pussey and thighs were well lathered by our love juices. Then he pulled out his shrunken penis, rubbing his shaft amorously in a last salute against my sticky cunney lips.

I looked at my bracelet watch and told the young scamp we had better dress ourselves and go downstairs to await the return of our parents. This we did, which was just as well, for not ten minutes later they came back to find Toby reading a newspaper and me playing the piano in the drawing room.

I do feel somewhat ashamed at fucking my young cousin, but he wanted it even more than I, for unwanted virginity is a most troublesome complaint. So where can there be any harm in this dalliance, especially as I do not intend to repeat the performance now that Toby has lost his cherry, to coin the expressive if rather vulgar American phrase.

As always, dear David, I would welcome your honest opinion on the matter, for you are one of the few people I can rely upon to give me an unbiased view on personal matters.

With all my love,
Angela

I did not have to wait long to find out what advice had been given to Angela Stomson for, as I folded the sheets of this letter and stuffed them back inside the envelope, I noticed another crumpled sheet of paper in the dictionary. With a smile of satisfaction, I opened it out and discovered that it turned out to be a carbon copy of the bookseller's typewritten reply to her *cri de coeur*, and it was with interest that I perused his reply which was as follows:

Dearest Angela,

My thanks for your letter and I take it as the greatest of compliments that you entrust me with your intimate thoughts. As you have stated, your cousin was delighted to have crossed the Rubicon into manhood and you will have earned his undying gratitude by guiding him on this occasionally perilous journey.

First love can be idyllic or quite disastrous and in later years, Toby will consider himself extremely fortunate to have been initiated into the pleasures of love-making. It is a time-honoured tradition that older women make the best partners for shy young virgin boys, although fifteen is not that young (after all, there is only two years difference in your ages) and he was obviously sexually competent and you were each turned on by the other, so all in all, I am sure that the experience will have been of mutual benefit, although I am equally certain that you are very wise not to continue the relationship.

I well recall the gossip a few years ago over a very similar state of affairs which involved Briony, Lord McBain's daughter and Oliver, the son of Sir Jonathan and Lady Abigail Letchmore. She was twenty-seven and he was sixteen. Whilst Oliver was a handsome boy and well-built for his age, the affair was doomed by infatuation. Whilst Briony felt more in control of the relationship with a younger man after a passionate sexual involvement with Colonel Bronzite (who, as you may know, is well-known in and around Mayfair for his robust sexual proclivities), alas, her entanglement with young Oliver also ended in mutual recrimination.

The draft ended at this point and I decided to destroy the letter, a fair copy of which I assumed had been posted in reply to Angela Stomson. I tore it up into little pieces and dropped them into the waste-paper basket and then wrote a short note to Mr Blow, enclosing Angela's letter to him, explaining how it had arrived in my hands and, after a pause for thought, I must confess that I decided to tell a white lie. Crossing the fingers of my left hand, I went on to assure him that although the envelope had been opened, to the best of my knowledge the letter had not been read! I salved my conscience by telling myself that if one of Mr Blow's assistants had not been so careless, this incriminating material would never have fallen into my hands and that it was fortunate that only I had seen the letters and not someone caddish enough to ask either party for money to restore the correspondence to its rightful owner.

At the same time, to soften the blow (please pardon the pun!) I ordered a copy of *Modern Daughters* by Miss Anne Fox-Smythe, the daring new book of conversations with girls of all classes on the foolish restrictions bound upon them by Society. Profusely illustrated with photographs and elegantly bound in silk cloth, the book will make an ideal present for Lord Gordon MacChesney, my old rogue of an uncle, who still has old-fashioned ideas about the place of women, a subject about which he is solely concerned in that every night there should be an attractive female between himself and the mattress!

CHAPTER TWO

Some Forbidden Escapades

What a difference the railway and the internal combustion engine have made to our social habits! Journeys which took my grandparents a fortnight can now be easily accomplished in a day. How much more pleasant it is to relax in the luxury of a first class carriage on a Southern Railways express where one can stretch one's legs, partake of refreshments, read a book or simply stare out of the window than to be jolted up and down inside a cold, cramped coach! And now even most minor roads are metalled, if not tarred, so that travelling by motor-car is so much nicer than bumping along rutted roads.

Nevertheless, although I could have travelled to Meverson Hall in one day, I decided to break my journey in London and, in the morning, Dennison and myself caught the early train to London and, as arranged, the Savoy had a motor car and driver waiting to meet us at Victoria Station.

By a happy coincidence, in the lobby of the hotel, whom should I meet but Mademoiselle Nicole Coulandre, another old friend from Madame Dupont's Academy in Lucerne.

'Rosie! How wonderful to see you!' she cried out in her sensually accented English. 'Normally I would have written to you to say I am coming to England, but we are staying only two days before journeying up to Newcastle where we will take a ship to Copenhagen to visit my sister Françoise who, as you may remember, married a Danish boy.'

Nicole was the daughter of a wealthy and well-connected family of wine-growers from the Bordeaux region and on my birthday, without fail she would send a case of chateau-bottled claret to Argosse Towers. In return, on her birthday (which was only six weeks before this chance meeting) I would reciprocate by ordering from Selfridge's their best Irish table linen of which she was very fond, and this year I had sent her a hemstitched and hand-embroidered bedspread which, according to her letter of thanks, she had adored.

I must mention here that she was perhaps the most beautiful of all the girls attending Madame Dupont's establishment. She was stunningly pretty with waist-length, liquorice-black hair and ice-blue eyes, an aristocratic, aquiline nose and full, sensuous lips. Nicole spoke impeccable English (her maternal grandmother hailed from Devon) and she and I had become close friends almost from the moment we first met, recognising a shared sense of humour and a taste for adventure not immediately apparent in many of our fellow students.

We fell into each other's arms and Nicole asked me what my plans were for the day. 'My parents have gone to the British Museum for the day,' explained the lovely girl, 'but I have arranged to meet Sir David Pickering after luncheon and he has promised to take me to the famous Jim Jam Club to see one of their naughty Victor Pudendum exhibitions.'

[*The Jim Jam Club in Great Windmill Street was a raffish establishment for upper crust Society gentlemen where all kinds of erotic entertainment took place during its heyday between the mid-1890s and 1914. Many underground magazines, including* The Oyster *and* The Rupert Mountjoy Diaries *make mention of the club which was secretly*

*patronised by King Edward VII and many of his cronies —
Editor*]

'I'm sure your parents don't know about *that*
arrangement,' I laughed and Nicole nodded and went on:
'No, they think he is taking me to an afternoon concert at
the Queen's Hall!

'Oh Rosie, it is good to see you again! Can you join me
for luncheon? And of course, if you are free, you are very
welcome to join Sir David and myself at the Jim Jam Club.'

'I don't know about that, Nicole,' I replied doubtfully
as we strode arm-in-arm down the corridor, 'but I'll happily
join you for luncheon.'

We ate a light meal of consommé, lamb steak marinated
in lemon and garlic and a fresh fruit salad which was quite
delicious and gave the lie to the old canard about our
restaurants only being able to offer solid English fare,
although I had to admit to Nicole that the Savoy chef was
in all probability a Frenchman!

'I'm really looking forward to seeing this Victor
Pudendum exhibition of fucking,' Nicole confided to me
as we walked into the lounge to have our coffee. Alas, we
had only sat down for a moment when a page-boy came up
to her with a message from Sir David Pickering, apologising
profusely for the short notice but regretting that he would
be unable to take her to the Jim Jam Club that afternoon
as his Aunt Maud had been taken ill and he felt it necessary
to rush down to Bournemouth to be at her bedside.

'Damn, that puts paid to my afternoon,' she said crossly.
'I would suggest that we went together, but I understand
that only members are allowed to attend, and they can only
bring two guests to a Victor Pudendum show.'

'Never mind,' I said, squeezing her arm, 'there'll always
be another opportunity. Look, after you have visited your
sister in Denmark, are you going home via London? If you
are, I am sure that Lord Philip Pelham is a member of the

Jim Jam Club and he will be pleased to escort us both to next month's Victor Pudendum contest.'

'What a splendid idea, Rosie! Yes, we will be back in London for three whole days from the seventeenth of July, but won't you be out of town during the summer?'

'Yes, but we shall not be travelling to France until the last week of July and the building work on our London house will be finished by then, so I can stay there,' I replied and Nicole leaned over and gave me a little kiss on the cheek.

Then she rummaged unsuccessfully in her bag for a notebook and said: '*Zut*, I have left my diary in my bedroom. I tell you what, though, come up to my room and I will write in our arrangement. Also, I would like you to taste some of the delicious cognac Gerard gave me as a leaving present before we left Bordeaux.'

'Who is Gerard?' I queried, and Nicole smiled as we rose and walked out towards the staircase. 'Gerard Leclerc is a nephew of one of our neighbours,' she explained. 'He is a very nice boy who has declared his undying love for me, but such are the strange ways of the heart, I cannot reciprocate his affections and whilst I have been tempted to surrender myself to him, I am sure you will agree, Rosie, that it is wrong to let a man fuck you simply out of pity for him. However, Gerard showers me with gifts and he insisted that I take a bottle of cognac with me on my travels, for medicinal purposes as well as for pleasure.'

Once in her room, Nicole made a note in her diary of our arrangement and then she opened her trunk and passed me a copy of *La Vie Folâtre* which I browsed through whilst she poured out two glasses of her boyfriend's cognac for us.

This very naughty magazine was full of the most lascivious photographs imaginable taken by 'Monsieur Jean-Paul, the well-known photographic artist whose work is reputedly collected by both His Majesty King Edward VII and the up-and-coming Mr Lloyd-George. The photographs showed naked young men and women with their cocks, pussies and bottoms freely displayed as they frigged, sucked and fucked each other in all kinds of ways and my blood began to warm as I looked at these sensual works of art.

Perhaps my favourite photograph was of a beautiful, dark-skinned African girl seated on the lap of her lover — but she had lifted her bottom just enough so that one could see that his thick, stiff shaft was already half embedded inside her cunt. Her arms were around his neck and her face was turned up, beaming with the satisfaction she was experiencing in her well-filled cunney.

Another showed two pretty nude girls in a clinch, their bodies pressed tightly together with their arms round their partner's waist and pressing the other's soft, rounded bottom. Each had a little finger slipped inside the cleft between the other's chubby bum cheeks.

'Does that picture excite you? Look at her luscious lips, her aroused nipples, she is lost in those first exquisite moments of a lovely fuck,' said Nicole softly as she handed me a glass of cognac. I sipped at the fiery liquid and then watched the lovely French lass toss her drink down in one gulp.

'I like the look of her as well,' I said hoarsely, and before I could say any more, the sweet girl nimbly unbuttoned my blouse and as if in a trance I unbuttoned my cuffs to allow her to slide the garment from my shoulders. We gazed at each other in silence for a moment and she whispered quietly: 'Shall we continue?'

I nodded my head and then we began to tear off all our clothes until we both stood naked. I placed my hands on Nicole's shoulders as she wriggled towards me and looked with delight at her elegant, slim body. We slid into an embrace and staggered drunkenly towards the bed, onto which we threw ourselves and began to kiss and cuddle. Brushing my palm against her stalky red nipples, I saw them swell and stand up proudly as I traced the slight curve of Nicole's stomach until my fingers became entangled in the thick dark curls of her bush. As our tongues waggled inside each other's mouths we sinuously rubbed our bodies together.

'You be the gentleman, *ma chérie*,' gasped Nicole as she lay on her back with her legs wide apart, and I gave my assent to her request by running my hand through the glossy pussey curls one more time before bending forward to flick my tongue against her large, erect, strawberry-coloured nipples which made her moan with delight. She pushed my head downwards until my face was buried between her thighs, and I kissed her moistening slit, licking and lapping at her sopping muff. Now, from the serrated vermilion lips, out popped Nicole's stiff, rubbery clitty, as big as a thumb. I opened her love lips further with my fingers and passed the tip of my tongue lasciviously up and down her juicy crack before taking her clitty in my mouth and playfully nipping it with my teeth. She wriggled deliciously and with a cry of: 'Oooh! Aaah! You are making me come, darling Rosie!' she spent profusely all over my mouth and chin.

We changed places and Nicole lay on top of me and, running her wet, pink tongue over her lips, she gently took one of my breasts in each hand and lowered her face to my nipples whilst with her clever fingers she opened my crack as wide as possible and then, directing her clitty at the pouting opening of my cunt, she somehow managed to stuff the hard, erectile flesh between my cunney lips, holding them tightly together with her hand. This kind of intra-feminine fucking was quite novel to me and I found it tremendously stimulating to have her clitty inside me.

In no time at all my cuntal juices were flowing freely as Nicole continued remorselessly to fuck my pussey, adding one, two and then three fingers until I felt the first faint waves of orgasm start deep inside me. These soon began to spread, setting every nerve on fire with intense pleasure, and I cried out with joy as I discharged a flood of love juice over her hand and over my thighs.

I stayed with Nicole until three o'clock and then we decided to dress and attend an afternoon concert arranged by the generous philanthropist, Sir Ronnie Dunn, in aid of the East End Milk Fund just a short taxi ride away at the Connaught Rooms. The Mayfair String Quartet which provided the entertainment was made up of four of the most gifted amateur musicians in London. The Quartet was led by the Honourable Jonathan Crawford, younger son of Viscount Sevenoaks and included Mr Peter Lucas, a popular young man-about-town, on second violin whilst the viola was in the capable hands of Miss Caroline Connor, the talented young niece of the Canadian High Commissioner and the group was completed by Dr Jonathan Abigaille, the popular Society physician whom gossip has involved with Lady Gaiman and Fiona Davidson, the prettiest of this year's crop of débutantes presented at Court. His mastery of the 'cello is less well-known although, as I later found out from Miss Connor, for the last three years he has been studying with the maestro Ludwig Seligsohn in Paris.

The large room was packed with the cream of Society and amongst the guests I recognised from the pages of *The Illustrated London News* were Mrs Michael Reynolds, Lady Shella de Souza and Mr Andrew Edwards, the immensely wealthy Kentish landowner reputed to possess one of the most enormous penises in all Europe, if one may believe his biographical details which were published in the latest scurrilous edition of *The Oyster*.

Nicole and I took our seats and after a few introductory words from Sir Ronnie Dunn, the musicians took the stage. The first piece of music on the programme was Haydn's gravely thoughtful String Quartet in F Sharp minor, an emotive and unusual key little used by the classical composers. Indeed, so little is composed in F Sharp minor that in more than six hundred works, Mozart only wrote one movement in it. However, as any of my musical readers will know, the stern opening to the Quartet soon modulates to a warmer A major before reverting back to the original key at the end of the first movement. I closed my eyes and enjoyed the music which was followed by Schubert's 'Death and the Maiden' Quartet and, after the interval for tea, the musicians were joined by the professional clarinettist Simon Kunowski for Brahms' heavenly Quintet in B Minor for Clarinet and Strings.

After the concert I was approached by Mr Edwards, a handsome gentleman in his early thirties, who bowed as he said: 'You are Miss Rosie d'Argosse, are you not? Perhaps you don't remember me but my name is Andrew Edwards and we were introduced by Lady Beckmann at the Marquis de Soveral's banquet at the Portuguese Embassy last October.'

Truthfully, I did not remember the introduction at which my father represented the Foreign Office, but I had no desire to hurt his feelings, so I flashed him a smile and said: 'Of course I remember you, Mr Edwards. And may I present you to my friend Mademoiselle Nicole Coulandre from Bordeaux.'

'*Enchanté, mademoiselle,*' he said, taking Nicole's hand and kissing her fingers in Continental style as he added shyly: 'But I'm ashamed to say that my French will not take me much further.'

Nicole fluttered her long eyelashes at Andrew Edwards' merry brown eyes and wide, generous lips and I could see that there was an instant attraction between the pair. She replied in her throaty Continental voice: 'That will be of no importance, Mr Edwards, because I wish to practise my English whilst I am in London.'

I will not bother to record the full details of what happened during the next hour but as soon as we could, we left the Connaught Rooms with Andrew who guided us towards his Rolls-Royce motor car which was standing just a few yards from the entrance. His chauffeur opened the doors for us and we drove back to the Savoy in style.

We went into the bar where he insisted on ordering a bottle of champagne. 'After all, it is my birthday tomorrow,' he said with a grin as we toasted his birthday in a superb Moet et Chandon '02 vintage. Then we toasted the *Entente Cordiale* [*the friendly treaty between Britain and France reached in April, 1904 which settled all outstanding colonial disputes between the two countries — Editor*], Nicole, myself, the Savoy Hotel and others which frankly I cannot remember!

However, I do remember that we adjourned to Nicole's suite after she had invited Andrew to taste the cognac which we girls had already downed before we left the hotel for the concert. After we had again toasted Andrew's birthday, Nicole's eyes lit up and she said: 'Rosie, come inside the dressing room for a moment. Andrew, please excuse us for a minute but I have just thought of a lovely birthday present for you. Would you like to take off your jacket, shoes and socks and turn and face the door.'

Slightly puzzled, I followed her into the small ante-room and she whispered to me: 'I know exactly the kind of gift that Andrew would appreciate,' as she kicked off her shoes. 'Come on, take off your clothes!'

She then told me of her plan and at first I demurred, but Nicole did not find it too difficult to make me change my mind! We both stripped to the buff and we peeked through the slightly open door to make sure that Andrew was following Nicole's instructions. Then we crept up on tip-toe behind him and Nicole reached up and covered his eyes with her hands.

'Are you ready for your surprise?' she asked with a giggle.

'Just about,' he said with a mixture of amusement and trepidation in his voice.

Nicole removed her hands and spun Andrew round so that he was treated to the sight of two beautiful girls, both stark naked, singing:

> *Happy birthday to you,*
> *Happy birthday to you,*
> *Happy birthday dear Andrew,*
> *Happy birthday to you!*

Andrew's jaw slackened and he blinked in disbelief at the sight of our glorious nude bodies. His chest heaved as his breathing quickened as his eyes darted from Nicole to me and back again, and his senses were obviously stirred by the sight of our pert, jiggling breasts, our peachy bottoms and hairy pussies as we danced gaily around him.

'Well now, Rosie informed me earlier this afternoon at the concert that in *The Oyster* it was reported you were given a five-star rating for fucking by the ladies at the Jim Jam Club,' said Nicole boldly, letting her hand brush across the front of Andrew's trousers where a noticeable swell had swiftly appeared. 'The point is, we want to give you something very special on your birthday, but we would not want to upset you by our little gift. Perhaps you can guess what it is, so if you would prefer not to receive it, do speak out now and I promise we will not be offended.'

'Oh, there's not the slightest danger of my being anything but delighted by whatever you have in mind,' said Andrew with a wolfish grin as I began to unbutton his shirt and Nicole unbuckled the smart leather belt around the waist of his trousers.

It took only a minute to divest our companion of all his clothing except for his drawers, and Nicole dropped to her knees and tugged them down to his feet. As she did so, his released thick shaft sprang up as if on a spring to stand up erect against his flat belly, rising majestically out of a mossy nest of crinkly hair under which dangled a pair of heavy-looking balls in their wrinkled, pink sack.

'*Alors*, this is a truly magnificent cock,' said Nicole with admiration as she grasped this twitching love truncheon in both hands. 'Does it taste as good as it looks?'

'This I cannot tell you,' replied Andrew as he pulled her head towards him. 'You will have to find out the answer for yourself.'

She wet her lips with her tongue as she cupped his hairy ballsack in her left hand whilst lightly running the fingers of her right hand up and down the muscular, ivory shaft of his massive penis.

'Is that nice, Andrew?' she asked rhetorically and when he gasped out his affirmation the naughty minx added mischievously: 'Well, if the wrapping paper is to your liking, come and see what's inside the box,' and Nicole pulled him by his prick towards the bed. They lay down together and their two faces moved closer until, closing their eyes, their lips met in a frenetic kiss, the moisture spreading as if they were eating a soft fruit which melted and dissolved as their tongues swished around in each other's mouths.

Andrew broke away from this embrace to move his lips down towards her thrusting nipple, running the tip of his tongue with surprising delicacy around the sensitive, encircling areole before cupping her breast in his hand and taking the erect tittie between his teeth and playfully nipping it, which caused the hot-blooded girl to squirm with new-found passion.

In the meantime, Nicole continued to massage his hot, smooth cock as Andrew's hand now glided across her dark pubic bush and spread the lips of her cunney.

'Nicole, your pussey is sopping wet — are you ready to

take my tadger inside your cunney?' he grunted, and she panted: 'Yes, oh yes, Andrew, slide that fat staff inside my cunt, you big-cocked boy!'

It did cross my mind as to whether Nicole would be able to accommodate such a thick pole as Andrew grinned and rolled the sweet girl onto her back, his hands slipping under her to grasp hold of her gorgeous bum cheeks as he lowered himself slowly upon her. The tip of his knob just touched her pouting pink cunney lips and he hesitated to plunge forward until Nicole repeated her demand to be fucked. Then he pressed home, inserting the domed helmet inside her honeypot, and her love tunnel miraculously expanded to take in his giant boner and he continued to push forward, inch by inch, until their pubic hairs were intermingled.

Nicole rotated her pretty backside around the fulcrum of his throbbing tool and she whimpered in appreciation as Andrew withdrew some three inches of his meaty shaft and then plunged forward again to the hilt. He continued this delicious movement until the length of his prick was glistening with the lubrication of Nicole's cuntal juices.

'Oooh! Oooh! *C'est magnifique!*!' she cried out as he increased the pace, his balls banging against her bottom with each lunging thrust, and as he lunged forward he gasped in a voice husky with lust: '*There*, can you feel my cock reaming out your pussey?'

'Yes, yes, YES!' she screamed as he added his fingers to rub her clitty whilst he continued to pound his enormous rampant rod in and out of her squelchy slit. Nicole trembled as she twisted and turned until her body stiffened and she screamed out: 'I'm coming! I'm coming! Quick, flood my cunt with spunk! Now!'

Andrew's cock fairly vibrated as it slid in and out of her juicy crack faster and faster until, with a hoarse cry, he jetted a torrent of frothy white spunk inside her love sheath which mingled with her own flood of tangy spend, and Nicole sighed with sheer bliss as they dissolved into the mutual glow which accompanies such a fervent fuck.

'Now, what else would you like for your birthday?' cooed Nicole and as he pondered the question I joined the lewd couple on the bed. He thought for a moment and then replied: 'Well now, Nicole, what would be very nice is to see you kiss Rosie's blonde-haired pussey. Would you humour my fancy, assuming of course that Rosie has no objection.'

'Far from it,' I replied, not offering the information that Nicole and I had already explored each other's bodies earlier in the afternoon. 'I adore being sucked off so much that I hardly care who is doing it. Indeed, for what it is worth, girls are far more adept at eating pussey than men.'

Andrew had ejaculated so violently into Nicole's willing womb that his prick was at half-mast (though even in this state it was bigger than many fully erect organs I have seen in my three years of active fucking), but his member twitched as, in a flash, Nicole and I began to cuddle up together and her hand snaked out to insert itself between my legs. I returned the embrace and she snuggled up even closer to me, brushing her face against mine as her other hand slid round my shoulder.

'M'mm, what lovely silky yellow hair you have, Rosie, and such beautiful pink cunney lips too! I'm sure they are wider than mine,' sighed Nicole as she rubbed her palm against the entrance to my pussey. I lay back to savour the exquisite feeling as she murmured: 'Part your legs a little wider, my darling, and bend your knees and then you can rub yourself off on my hand.'

I followed her instructions and I saw Andrew Edwards' cock twitch again as I worked my furry love lips upon the heel of her palm, forward and back again, increasing the speed as my excitement grew steadily and the love juices began to drip down onto my thighs.

With a low growl, Nicole now raised her thumb, causing it to caress my clitty with each forward bumping of my hips, so that my head began to swirl and I moaned and worked my bottom faster whilst Nicole increased the pace of the circling with her thumb. This wonderful frigging brought down a flood of cuntal juices and I swam in a sea of lubricosity as deep quivers of ecstasy charged through my body and I spurted my spend on Nicole's hand whilst Andrew scrambled to his knees and presented the uncapped knob of his huge cock to my mouth. I lapped at the glowing helmet with my tongue, tasting his salty 'pre-cum' as my warm fingers tried to encircle his tremendous tool, but I needed both hands to do so. I moved my head downwards to lick his balls and my nostrils were filled with his distinctive musky maleness. Lightly, I ran my tongue from the base to the tip of his cock and back again as he groaned with delight. Then, in one sinuous movement, I opened my mouth as wide as possible and took in as much of his stupendous shaft as possible between my lips. I could only manage to suck in about half the length of his big boner but I enjoyed the experience and I sucked strongly and rhythmically whilst my gentle fingers stroked and tickled his wrinkly ballsack.

Then, seeing that try as I may I was having some difficulty with his over-large member, he withdrew and whispered to me to get up on my knees and face the wall. I did as I was told and held on to the head-board and I bent forward with my legs slightly apart and my bum cheeks stuck out provocatively, waiting for Andrew to split them with his immense cock. I did not have long to wait and I felt the lusty man guide his pulsing prick into my cunt from behind. He slewed his shaft in and out forcefully, whilst Nicole ducked her head between his legs and sucked one of his balls inside her mouth whilst she frigged her own pussey in time with Andrew's shaft as it moved backwards and forwards in the narrow crevice between my buttocks. He wrapped his arms tightly around me and his hands cupped my breasts, and this proved such a stimulating experience that very soon we spent almost simultaneously, and I thrilled to the power of the electric shocks that crackled out from my cunney as Andrew spunked copiously inside my tingling love tunnel.

The three of us fell back exhausted onto the pillows, but when we had recovered, Andrew invited us to dine at his rooms that evening (he kept a small suite in one of the new blocks of apartments in Park Lane). 'My sister Gwendolen will be there and if you ladies play bridge, after dinner we could play a few rubbers.'

We accepted his offer with genuine pleasure for we were both keen bridge players. Nicole played with great flair although she was wont to over-value her hand, and I remember once reminding her of the anecdote told by my parents who were playing against His Majesty and Mrs Keppel. Our Monarch bid outrageously and when as dummy he put down his hand for his partner to play the round, Mrs Keppel blanched and said: 'Sire, all I can say about this contract is God save the King because the cards won't!'

As it happened, the cards favoured me and I won every rubber with whoever partnered me. 'Lucky in cards, unlucky in love,' I sighed, but Andrew rebuked me and said robustly: 'Nonsense, Rosie, a girl like you can have her pick of all the most handsome bachelors in town.'

The next morning I bade farewell to Nicole and the hotel motor-car took Dennison and me to Paddington where we caught the express train to Cardiff. I have always enjoyed travelling on the railway. Even when I was a little girl I never used to draw back from the edge of the platform when the engine came huffing and puffing into Midhurst station. Also, as my diary will show, I have enjoyed some marvellous fucking in railway carriages (although it is preferable to have

69

a private compartment for privacy). [*see 'Rosie 2 — Young Wild and Willing — Editor*]

Yet I can truthfully say that sensuous adventures were far from my mind as Dennison opened the door of the first class ladies-only carriage. 'Are all the bags safely on board?' I asked and after he assured me that he had personally seen the porter stow our cases in the guard's van, he shut the door and made his way to his reserved seat in the second-class section of the train. Unlike most of our neighbours who book their servants third class, we always allow our staff to relax in the more comfortable second-class seats.

'We're stopping at Bath and Bristol, Miss Rosie. Shall I come by at Bristol to see if there's anything you need?' said my footman.

'Thank you, that won't be necessary, Dennison,' I answered, handing him my morning paper which had little news that was of interest to me. 'I have a bell to call for an attendant if necessary. Enjoy the trip and I'll see you in Cardiff.'

'Very good, Miss,' he said as he retired and I sat down alone in the compartment. But as I settled into my seat I noticed that opposite me, two of the other seats had 'reserved' labels attached to them. I looked at my watch — the ladies who had booked these seats had better hurry because the train would leave in less than five minutes.

I opened the novel which I had purchased from the W. H. Smith station bookstall and had just started to read the first page, when the door from the corridor burst open and in came the two late arrivals.

'Rosie d'Argosse! Fancy seeing you here,' said a familiar voice, and I looked up to see that one of the two young ladies who had entered the compartment was none other than an attractive girl of my own age whom I had met at Lord Philip Pelham's birthday party some six or seven weeks before.

70

Frantically I searched the recesses of my brain for her name and fortunately I recalled it in time to spare any blush of embarrassment. 'Hello there, it's Vicky Clipstone, isn't it? How are you keeping?'

'Very well, thank you,' said Vicky and she turned to her companion and said: 'Sheila, this is Miss Rosie d'Argosse. Rosie, meet my cousin Miss Sheila Collingham.'

We shook hands and as the station-master blew his whistle and the train lurched forward, I said to Vicky: 'How nice to see you again. I don't suppose we are travelling to the same destination by any chance.'

'We've been invited for a few days' tennis in the wilds of rural Wales by a girl Sheila and I have known since we were very young,' she replied, and I said with a smile: 'Not Susannah Meverson by any chance?'

'Yes, that's right. Why, don't tell me you have been invited, too? How jolly! But if I remember rightly, you live in Sussex, don't you Rosie? How do you come to know the Meversons?'

I explained that Susannah and I were old friends and Vicky said: 'Of course! When we met at Phil Pelham's party you told me that you spent four years at St Hilda's and that's where you first came across that handsome young man Robert Bacon who was chatting to us before dinner.'

At the mention of Robert's name, Vicky's cousin blushed a bright crimson and I looked more closely at the pretty young girl who could have been little more than sweet seventeen. She was extremely pretty, being of a light complexion, rather slender of figure but with well-proportioned breasts and hazel eyes.

Vicky was of my age, some two or three years older and she was a lovely rosy-cheeked girl with a merry twinkle in her blue eyes, which were of a similar shade to mine, although her strawberry blonde hair was two or three shades lighter than mine (I don't believe I have mentioned before

71

that my colouring comes from my maternal Swedish grandmother).

Anyway, Vicky also noticed the change of colour in her cousin's face and she winked at me as she said: 'Now, now, Sheila, you don't have to worry. Even as we speak, Robert is boarding the *S.S. Mauretania* and will be in New York for the next three months. Did you know that, Rosie?'

With a nod, I replied: 'Yes, Robert telephoned me to tell me about it last week. He was only given a week's notice but his uncle, Lord Richmond, is indisposed and so Robert will represent the Bacon and Wright merchant bank at some important business meetings. It will be his first visit to America and he sounded very excited about the trip.'

'There, so you see there is no call for you to be concerned,' said Vicky to her young cousin. She could see that I was curious to know why Robert's presence might embarrass Sheila and she said: 'It's all too ridiculous for words, Rosie, but the fact of the matter is that after dinner at Phil Pelham's, Sheila and Robert went upstairs to the music room.'

I raised my eyebrows at this remark because only a day or so before the party, Philip was chuckling about the fact that he had arranged for a few honoured guests who required privacy to be given keys to any of the several unused rooms in his imposing town house in Belgrave Square.

'I can't believe that Robert acted in a caddish way towards you,' I remarked with some feeling. 'In my experience [*see 'Rosie 2: Young Wild and Willing' — Editor*] he is a perfect gentleman.'

'Quite so, and that evening Robert did nothing underhand,' said Vicky robustly. 'Look, Rosie, I know that you can be trusted to keep a secret. What concerns my dear cousin is the fact that — well, Sheila, you tell Rosie yourself about what happened between you and Robert. Don't be

72

shy, I know that you may speak to her in complete confidence and if she confirms what I have told you, then perhaps you'll stop worrying about it.'

The young girl's cheeks coloured up again and she wriggled uncomfortably in her seat, but she decided to take this advice for she said: 'Yes, I trust you, Miss d'Argosse, as Robert mentioned to me at the party that you and he were acquainted and he said some very nice things about you.'

'How nice! And I am only too happy to return his compliments,' I said with an easy smile. 'Now then, tell me how I can help you.'

She lowered her eyes and said: 'Well, the very moment that I set eyes on Robert Bacon, my heart began pounding. Perhaps it was his handsome face, the set of his muscular shoulders or the clearness of his deep blue eyes that raked the gathering with a predatory gaze as he cut through the crowd of girls who flocked around him with the cool assurance of a panther stalking its prey. I could hardly believe my luck when I was placed next to Robert at dinner and I found him a most agreeable companion, so easy to talk to and during the course of our conversation, we discovered that we had several interests in common. One of these interests was sport and Robert was rather taken with the fact that I was keen on cricket.'

Sheila paused and I said encouragingly, 'Yes, of course, Robert was captain of cricket at St Trippett's school and won his cricket blue at Oxford. He now plays for *I Zingari* and whenever time allows, turns out for the Kent county side.'

'He is a talented all-round sportsman,' she agreed with an animated expression on her face. 'And did you know that he also won his University colours for soccer and hockey as well?'

Oh-ho, it was becoming very clear that Sheila had been

smitten by Robert Bacon, which was hardly surprising for he was after all a noted Lothario, but I said nothing and waited for her to continue.

'I don't deny that I was very attracted to Robert and when after dinner he suggested that we went to look at Lord Pelham's sporting prints in the music room, I knew what he meant — but I went! Well, of course, we didn't waste too much time looking at Phil Pelham's pictures and in minutes we were locked together in a passionate embrace on a sofa. I was wearing a low-cut evening dress and oh my, I felt so frisky when Robert moved his hands from my back to rove over my scantily covered bosom, and I made no objection when he unhooked the top of my dress and pulled out my bare breasts. I nearly swooned with delight.

'He kissed and sucked my titties, making them stand up like little red soldiers and even though I knew I should have protested, I made no attempt to stop him when he placed his hand on my knee and started to work it up my leg. I even let him slip his fingers inside my knickers and allowed them to toy with my dampening bush.

'We continued to kiss and cuddle in this way and when Robert placed my hand on the huge bulge in his lap, I eagerly squeezed the fat, stiff pole inside his trousers. He quickly unbuttoned his trousers and I plunged my hand inside and felt for his naked prick which sprang out like a Jack-in-the-box. I grasped hold of his hot, velvet-skinned shaft and began to slide my hand up and down it, capping and uncapping his big, wide knob. Now I had never taken a boy's cock in my mouth before but my lips were drawn as if by some invisible magnet to the mushroom-like helmet of Robert's lovely tadger. I kissed the smooth crown and then, after licking all round it, I opened my mouth and sucked his knob into my mouth.

'Ah, it tasted wonderful with a fine, masculine tang as I closed my lips round his shaft as firmly as possible and continued to work on his knob, washing it all over with my tongue. I tried to cram more of his throbbing tool inside my mouth and I almost choked in the attempt. "Don't try too hard," he whispered lovingly. "Here, let me rub your titties whilst you suck my prick," and he began to flick at my rock-hard nipples, exciting me even more as I sucked away with my hands cupping his hairy balls which I massaged gently, lifting and separating each from the other as I gobbled furiously on my fleshy sweetmeat, savouring the salty taste and he jerked his hips upwards, thrusting more of his slippery shaft deeper between my lips. "Oh my God, I'm coming!" he gasped and before I could even think of pulling away he shot his sticky cream down my throat and I swallowed his spunk in great gulps, sucking on his pulsating prick until I had milked it of all the contents of his big balls, and his shaft started to shrink back to its normal size.

'We went no further, which was just as well because there was a rattle at the door as some other couple tried to come in, but afterwards I could hardly look Robert in the eye when we rejoined the main group of guests. What would Robert think of my being so forward on the very first time of our meeting? And would he tell his friends about what I did, earning me an unwanted reputation as a hussy?'

The girl looked piteously at me and I took her hands in mine and gently squeezed them. 'Oh, Sheila, you are a silly billy!' I cried with total sincerity. 'Now I don't know what Vicky has said to you about the incident, but in my opinion Robert won't mention a word of what happened between the two of you to a living soul.

'To begin with, he is a gentleman and as such would never disclose the names of his lovers to a living soul. And frankly, as he would tell you himself, to find an English girl who obviously enjoys cock-sucking as much as you is a real joy. So many are led to believe that there is nothing more to fucking than lying back and letting the man do the familiar old in-and-out. Why, I can hardly begin to tell you how many of the gay blades around town would be on their bended knees if you would give them a — now what do the Americans call it — a "blow job" such as you have just described. Robert will want to keep you to himself, that's for sure, and so you have absolutely nothing in the world to worry about.'

'Do you really mean it, Rosie?' said Sheila hopefully, and I looked straight into her eyes as I answered: 'Yes, of course I do,' and Vicky added triumphantly: 'See, Sheila, what did I say? Rosie has confirmed exactly what I told you. Now will you stop worrying and enjoy yourself?'

She nodded and said gratefully: 'Oh, thank you both so much for listening to me. Now I can enjoy the next few days without a care in the world.' But then she clapped her hand over her mouth and said: 'Oh dear, there is something else I'm worried about — I don't think I reminded Elsie to pack my new tennis racquet!'

'You were far too busy thinking about Robert Bacon,' laughed Vicky. 'I guessed that you might forget something so I supervised the packing whilst you were writing a letter to your sister, Maud.'

Vicky turned to me and said: 'Have you brought any servants with you? We just have Elsie, one of our housemaids, accompanying us.'

I told them that Dennison was in one of the second-class carriages and then a conductor came into the compartment to clip our tickets and to see if we required any refreshments before luncheon. The three of us decided not to eat anything before the mid-day meal, which would be served at twelve-thirty, for we were due in Cardiff a little more than an hour and a half later.

'Would you like something saucy to read before luncheon, Rosie?' enquired Vicky as she opened her travelling bag. 'I have this month's copy of *The Oyster* if it is of interest.

Sheila is going to finish *The Rupert Mountjoy Memoirs* whilst I would like a little nap.'

'I did buy a book at the station, but I'd much rather read your naughty magazine,' I confessed, holding out my hand for the elegantly bound publication which, since being printed on art paper in Paris, could be taken for a learned journal with its plain dark blue cover.

I opened the latest edition of the best of our *sub rosa* periodicals at a fascinating letter by Colonel Piers Rankin of the Sixth Punjab Rifles on *The Beauties of the Bare Behind* in which he chided the editor of *The Oyster* for not showing more photographs of girls' backsides. For those readers who have not had the good fortune to read Colonel Rankin's essay, here is an abridged copy of what he had to say:

Sir,

In my opinion, the female backside has sadly been neglected in your selection of photographs for the monthly picture gallery. Several of the girls featured are the most admirable specimens of female pulchritude and I especially commend those of Misses Paxford, Robson and Walshaw in the January issue. Yet whilst admitting that pictures of face, breasts, thighs and pussey are to be commended, why ignore the twin voluptuous orbs of the buttocks which are so firm and yet so tender, so resilient and so inviting?

A girl's bum cheeks, perhaps more than any other part of her anatomy, transmit the results of a good fucking. In the heat of passion, these pneumatic spheres tremble and twitch with each thrust of the prick in a lusty language of sensuality which should be studied by all men who aspire to be great lovers.

So in your next issue, Mr Editor, let us see a girl with a nice rounded bottom. For preference, dress her up in a pair of stockings, because these accentuate the luxuriant curves of the bum very nicely. Perhaps she could be wearing a dress, but no knickers, and bend over with her dress pulled up showing her delicious behind and looking saucily over her shoulder as if to say: 'If you like what you see, come and get it!'

Another good pose would be to have the wench lying face down on the bed, pushing out her snowy white buttocks towards the camera with her thighs open just enough so that we might catch a look at her hairy crack.

Of course, I do not want you to omit any photographs which show the glories of the female form from the front! Your excellent magazine shows us many beauties that make my old pego almost burst out from my trousers. But do not forget confirmed lovers of the bum like myself who frequently search through the pages of The Oyster *for our most favoured poses with little or no success.*

I am, Sir, your honourable servant,
(Colonel) Piers Rankin M.C.
New Delhi, India

Underneath his letter was a short reply from the Editor:

I sincerely hope that the next two pages of photographs showing Miss Fiona Feltham-Hardie of East Croydon and Mr George Lucas of Bloomsbury will be of especial interest to the gallant Colonel, whose criticisms have been noted.

With a trembling hand I turned the page and drew a sharp breath as I looked at the superb photograph of young George Lucas, a popular guest at many a country house weekend, fucking a tall blonde girl from behind, sliding his thick prick between her pert bum cheeks as she stood upright with her hands against a wall with her bottom thrust out. In the next picture, taken from a side angle, dear Lucas was seen rubbing his fingers over her high tilted breasts whilst her own hand was placed between her legs, tweaking her clitty and in a final photograph, taken after the actual fuck, George was shown on his knees licking out her spunk-filled cunney whilst Fiona stood with her head thrown back and her body arched back in ecstasy.

My pussey began to tingle as I studied the photographs, which I noticed had been taken by Count Gewirtz of Galicia, who was described quite recently in *The Times* as by far the most talented amateur photographer in all Europe. How I would have enjoyed being fucked by George Lucas, I thought to myself, but my reverie was broken by a knock on the door from the conductor who called out to us that luncheon would be served in five minutes.

With a heavy sigh, I tapped Vicky on the arm and gave the magazine back to her and then the three of us trooped out and went to the luncheon car where we ate a very good mayonnaise of salmon, and I chose an equally good roast chicken as my main course whilst my travelling companions opted for braised ox tongue. Although the roast potatoes were delicious, as usual in England, both the green vegetables were slightly overcooked and we were somewhat disappointed with the raspberry and currant tart, the pastry of which should have been lighter. But the bottle of claret we shared was very drinkable and all in all we could not grumble at the bill which worked out at exactly half a crown [*12½p! – Editor*] a head.

The large locomotive thundered into Cardiff dead on time and Dennison supervised the loading of Vicky's and Sheila's luggage along with my valises onto the local train for Carmarthen. We left at half past two and after leaving the grimy industrial heartland of South Wales, we trundled through the beautiful countryside at a gentle pace until we reached Carmarthen where Owen, the Meverson's chauffeur, was waiting with the family's splendid Mercedes motor car to transport us in fine style on the final stretch of our long journey to Meverson Hall some eight and a half miles away in the heart of the verdant Pembrokeshire countryside. A local van driver had been hired to bring on our servants and the luggage, which I am sure was not nearly as comfortable as the luxurious leather seats of the Mercedes Simplex, not one of the newest automobiles but certainly one of the most reliable. [*Rosie was a good judge of a motor car — in 1991 a Mercedes Simplex was bought at auction for more than two million dollars! — Editor*]

It was almost six o'clock when we reached the gates of Meverson Hall and Susannah was out in the drive with a young man whose face was vaguely familiar to me but whom at first I did not recognise.

'Hello, everyone, welcome to Wales!' she cried as she kissed all three of us in turn. 'How lovely to see you all! Now before we go any further, let me introduce Michael Harper to you.'

Susannah's mention of the name of her companion was enough to make further introduction unnecessary, for of course this good-looking fellow was none other than the famous tennis champion who is so popular at the Hurlingham Club, not only for his feats on court but also for his prowess in the bedroom. It is an open secret that he and Helena, the daughter of Lord Oxford, have long conducted a passionate if clandestine affair, whilst his name has also been linked to two older women, Mrs Charles Arbuthnot and Mrs Rayleigh de Berri, both of whom are supposed to have showered gifts upon the muscular young sportsman for his favours.

It was easy to see why women were so attracted to Michael Harper. He was slim and tall with a shock of curly chestnut hair, deep brown eyes with a straight nose and full, sensual lips. He was also fortunate enough to possess the most beautifully even set of white teeth and these were set off so well by his bronzed complexion, which he doubtless owed to the fact that his mother was of Italian ancestry, being the sister of the Duke of Padua.

We shook hands and, was it my imagination, but did Michael Harper hold my hand just a little longer than was necessary, and could I have misjudged the lingering caress of his fingers against mine as our eyes locked together?

'You three girls must be exhausted after your travels,' declared our kind hostess, escorting us up the steps of the impressively large mansion. 'Do come inside and have some refreshment. Your luggage should be here shortly and the staff will put your cases in your respective rooms.

'Our party is now complete,' Susannah informed us as I took a glass of white wine from the tray being offered round by a footman. 'The other three gentlemen arrived at noon and they went for a walk this afternoon.'

'Might I know any of them?' enquired Vicky, and Susannah shook her head. 'Probably not, although I am sure you will find them all quite charming. The first is one of Michael's friends from Oxford, Rodney Bakewell-Fisher, whose great passion in life is ornithology.'

'Oh, what a fortunate coincidence, did you know that I have taken up bird-watching since we last saw each other?' said Sheila shyly, and our hostess smiled and said: 'Certainly I knew, my love, your cousin told me and this was one of the reasons why I invited Mr Bakewell-Fisher to join us this weekend. Now the other two guests are Herr Oskar Gottlieb, a frightfully nice Jewish lawyer from Switzerland who works for old Tum-Tum's friend, Sir Ernest Cassel. [*'Tum-Tum' was the nickname given to the increasingly portly Edward VII by his cronies in the Marlborough House set, and Sir Ernest Cassel was the King's foremost financial adviser and close friend — Editor*] And the guest list will be completed by Lieutenant Christopher Cooney of the Household Cavalry. Lord Philip Pelham had planned to join us but, alas, he had a prior engagement.'

Vicky frowned and said: 'I think I have met Lieutenant Cooney, Susannah, but I can't quite recall the time and place. Wait a moment, could it have been at Lady Heather Dewsnap's coming-out ball in Cheltenham last summer?'

'Yes, you probably did — Christopher is a Dewsnap on his mother's side. Did you dance together by any chance?'

A rather odd little smile appeared on Vicky's lips but she shook her head and said mysteriously: 'Not exactly, but Christopher and I did engage in some intimate conversation.'

I resolved to ask her to explain this cryptic remark as Palmer the butler arrived to inform us that our luggage had arrived. I stood up but Susannah said: 'There's no rush, Rosie, we won't dine until half past eight tonight. Wouldn't you like to wait and meet Oskar and Christopher before you go upstairs? Oh, and there's something else I must say. You all remember that in my invitation I mentioned that my aunt, Lady Sheringham, was to be here to act as a chaperone in the absence of my parents. Well, unfortunately, dear Aunt Augusta has been laid low by an attack of influenza and is unable to move from her home.

'What a terrible shame,' she added ironically. 'If any of you ladies feel unsafe without Aunt Augusta prowling around the landing at night to make sure that there is no flitting between the rooms, of course I will understand if you want to return home tomorrow!'

We all laughed heartily as I made for the door. I wanted to take a bath before dinner, so I excused myself and Palmer showed me to my room where a maid had already opened my trunks and was busy hanging out my clothes. She bobbed a curtsy to me as I entered and said in a pleasing Welsh lilt: 'Good evening, ma'am, my name is Jenny, and I'll be looking after you whilst you are at Meverson Hall. There's a bell by the side of your bed if you need to call me or whoever is on duty.'

'Thank you, Jenny,' I said to the attractive slip of a girl, who was of about my own age with cornflower hair, light blue eyes, a tiny nose and lovely heart-shaped lips.

She stood there silently for a moment, fidgeting from side to side, and so I added: 'Don't let me disturb you, Jenny, I'll run my own bath whilst you finish unpacking,' but the girl still stood there looking flustered and tongue-tied as she fumbled with her apron.

'Is there something you want to ask me?' I said patiently, and finally she screwed up her courage and said: 'Excuse me, ma'am, I hope you don't mind my asking but did I catch a glimpse of Jack Dennison down in the servants' hall a few minutes ago?'

'Yes, he's my footman. Why do you ask? Have you two met before?'

Jenny nodded and said: 'Jack, I mean, Mr Dennison and I were in service together at Mr Duntocher's house in Gloucestershire before I left to come here and he took up service with you.

'I haven't seen him since,' she added, and from the tone of her voice I deduced that she was not exactly over-pleased to see my servant again.

I took her arm and pushed Jenny gently down on the bed. Then I sat myself down next to her and said softly: 'I think there's something bothering you about Dennison, isn't there? You can tell me about it if you like. I promise I won't repeat anything to Miss Meverson or any of the other guests.'

The petite little filly wriggled uncomfortably and murmured: 'You're ever so kind, ma'am, but it's such a rude story.'

'That doesn't matter at all,' I said in a cheerful tone, and I took her hand and went on: 'Jenny, you might have heard of Mrs Patrick Campbell, she's a very famous actress and a friend of the highest in the land. Well, she once remarked that she didn't care a damn how people wanted to fuck, just so long as they didn't do it in the street and frighten the horses!'

My words brought a smile to her face and she said: 'Did she really? Oh go on, she never did, did she?'

'She did,' I assured her, noting that Jenny had not turned a hair at my deliberately down-to-earth language. 'So don't be bashful, I'm a country girl myself and where I come from, we call a spade a spade.'

This gave the attractive girl more confidence and she told me how on one of her weekly half holidays, the rain was tumbling down outside so she spent the afternoon lying on her bed reading a copy of *The Oyster* which she had filched from the waste-bin in Mr Duntocher's study. She was reading about one of Sir Ronnie Dunn's horny adventures and as she put it: 'I became very excited when he wrote how he tore off Laura Bayswater's satin nightgown, leaving her naked and trembling on the bed and how, after ripping off his own clothes, he jumped on top of her and she grabbed his thick prick and pressed his knob between the damp lips of her juicy cunney . . .

'Almost unconsciously I allowed my hand to slip inside my blouse and I soon lowered my chemise and found my nipple and began to roll it between my fingers as my own pussey began to moisten. I continued to read, quite glued to the page as Sir Ronnie described how he kissed Laura's large red titties and then let his lips travel down to the neat little triangle of crisp brown hair which covered her mount.

'I shivered all over as I unbuttoned my skirt and pushed my hand into my knickers. My fingertips strayed towards my pussey and soon I started to slide them in and out of my love hole. Oooh, I felt so randy as I read on, with one set of fingers tweaking my tittie and with the other dipping my fingers in and out of my wet honeypot, rubbing my thumb against my clitty which always drives me wild.

'I was just building up to a spend when, I just don't know why, I almost jumped out of my skin when I looked up and saw that I was not alone! Jack Dennison was at the doorway, leaning against the wall and looking at me with a lust-laden expression on his face. I gasped and pulled down my skirt but he begged me to carry on. "Don't stop now, Jenny," he growled hoarsely. "I've seen so much already that it would be torture not to let me see you finish yourself off."

'All sorts of ideas now crossed my mind. I'd never played with myself in front of a man before and part of me felt terribly embarrassed — yet there was something weirdly exciting about knowing that Jack was there watching me, and from the bulge in his trousers I could see that his prick was hardening as he looked down at me. This very thought made me decide to continue, so I murmured: "Lock the door," which he did as I slowly began to undress, opening my blouse and pulling out one of my breasts from my chemise, letting it jut out proudly as I pulled down my knickers, threw up my skirt and spread my legs wide apart so that he could see the red chink of my cunt as I let my fingers stray through my bush.

'I closed my eyes and began to finger-fuck myself, taking my clitty and pressing its pink, shell-like firmness and I squeezed my legs together — oooh, I'm sorry, Miss, just thinking about it is making my knickers wet àgain!

'Then I heard a grunt coming from Jack's direction and I opened my eyes to see him standing there with his trousers down, rubbing his big stiff dick for all he was worth and each time he slid his fist up and down his shaft it made a squelchy sort of sound which made me even more excited.'

Jenny lowered her voice and went on: 'Jack's very well-made, if you know what I mean, ma'am. He's been blessed with the thickest prick I've ever seen and when he walked towards me and presented me with this shiny monster, I simply couldn't resist giving his knob a little kiss. He shuddered all over when I did this and moved even closer. I took his hot, hard cock in one hand as I continued to lick his helmet and with the other, I weighed his balls in my palm and then gently scraped them with my fingernails.

'This sent Jack wild and his prick bucked inside my mouth as I sucked in his knob between my lips. This made his shaft swell even more, especially when I grabbed his bum cheeks in my hands and pulled him even closer and took another three inches of his tool inside my mouth. I massaged the underside of his pole with my tongue, keeping my head still as Jack jerked his cock in and out until he went rigid and, with a groan, he spurted jets of sticky spunk which I gulped down as his shaft softened and he took it out of my mouth.

'Naturally, after he had recovered he begged to be allowed to fuck me. But I explained that it was too risky a time for that unless he had a Frenchie [*a condom – Editor*]. "I don't, but I swear that I won't spend inside you," he promised, but I'd known too many accidents playing *that* game and I shook my head. "I'll go through the tradesmen's entrance," he urged, but I have to be in the mood for bum-fucking and I didn't fancy it just then.

' "You'll just have to settle for a mutual sucking-off," I told him and to give him credit, he didn't try to force the issue. I positioned him on his knees in front of me between my legs and I parted them so that he could have a good look at my pouting pussey lips. Then I took his hand and placed it in the silky wet clump of cunney hair. His fingers splayed my love lips whilst the knuckles of his other hand ran down the full length of my gash. Then he pushed his fingertip inside my cunt and, as he penetrated my squishy slit, my hips rose to meet this miniature imitation cock.

'Oh, I really wanted his big, meaty prick there, but I knew I had to resist the temptation so slipped my fingers round his glistening wet shaft and lapped up the sticky jism which was already oozing from the tiny little hole in his knob.

'Then I tugged off my skirt and moved myself up over Jack until my pussey was over his nose, and he pulled me down and buried his face in my soaking bush, licking my cunney so beautifully that my love juice was soon dripping onto his lips and chin. My own lips were now as busy as his and I swirled my tongue all around his knob before cramming as much of his throbbing tool as I could into my mouth. I wrapped one hand round his hot shaft and sucked the smooth purple helmet, flicking the tip of my tongue over the slitted end whilst I cradled his balls through their crinkly covering of pink skin.

'It was all so exciting that we soon climaxed together, and my cum streamed out all over his face as he shot a frothy stream of creamy seed between my lips, so fiercely that the first jet hit the back of my throat. Honestly, ma'am, he spent so copiously that I could not swallow all his spunk and some of the jism dripped out of my mouth into the rough, wiry hair around the base of his cock.'

A smile of fond remembrance spread over the face of the young maid and I commented. 'Well, that all sounds very nice to me. Many people actually prefer a *soixante neuf* to a fuck. So why does Dennison's appearance in the servants' hall now distress you?'

She pouted prettily and said: 'He lost me my position, ma'am, because he peached upon me and the master to Mr Duntocher's aunt, Lady Clydebank.'

I looked at her questioningly and she explained: 'A few days after what I have just described took place, I was serving breakfast to Mr Duntocher. Unfortunately, I had overslept and had to be woken up by Mrs Cheatham, the housekeeper, and I was in such a hurry that I rushed downstairs to begin work without putting on any underclothes, and just before I served the master I looked in the mirror and I could see my nipples straining against the thin white cotton of my blouse. "Hurry up, Jenny, take in the bowl of fresh fruit to the dining room,'' called Mrs Cheatham, so there was no time to rush back upstairs and change. I took a deep breath and marched in, hoping that Mr Duntocher wouldn't take exception to looking at my titties.'

'I'm sure your master was far from displeased to catch even a glimpse of such a fine pair as yours, my dear,' I commented, running my hand across her high, uptilted breasts.

'Thank you, ma'am, and yes, in fact Mr Duntocher was so taken aback by the sight of my titties pressing against the almost transparent white material of my blouse that he dropped the toast-rack and its contents. When I bent down to help him pick up the toast he pinched my bottom and we ended up having a grand morning fuck on the dining-room table.

'From that morning on, I was being fucked every morning by Mr Duntocher and every evening by Jack Dennison. And that's where that fearful old cow Lady Clydebank, on whom Mr Duntocher depends for his annual allowance, comes into the picture. She disapproves of any familiarity, as she calls it, ''with members of the lower orders'', the cheeky old cow. Well, when she arrived at the house on an unexpected visit, Jack deliberately showed her into the dining room, knowing full well that at the time I was in there, down on my knees, gobbling the master's cock, and later that day I was told to pack my bags.'

This puzzled me and I asked: 'But why would Dennison want you to be sacked? After all, he was fucking you every night, wasn't he?'

Jenny shrugged her shoulders and replied: 'He was jealous about sharing my favours with the master, I suppose. Mr Duntocher didn't really want me to leave, but his aunt was adamant that unless I was out of the house in twenty-four hours she would stop his allowance. He wrote me a wonderful letter of reference, though, and gave me a ten pound note (that's six months' money) as a leaving present. Luckily, I was engaged at Meverson Hall a week later and I far prefer working here, so everything's turned out well. And the funny thing is, Lady Clydebank insisted that Mr Duntocher give all the servants notice as she decided they must all be infected with the same disease of immorality, and Dennison had to look for a new position. Now I know they say you must forgive people who trespass against you, but at the time I swore that I never wanted to see Jack Dennison again, and that still holds good.'

I sat down on the bed and said slowly: 'To be honest, Dennison has given my family excellent service since he has been in our employ, but if what you say is true, I shall have to look on him in a new light. Still, I'm glad you've informed me of your feelings.'

She continued to unpack my clothes whilst I went into the bathroom and switched off the taps. Whilst I lay in the bath I resolved that I would broach what I had heard with Dennison, because although we are of a more liberal persuasion than Lady Clydebank, I wouldn't be able to trust Dennison again until I heard his side of the story.

After my bath I decided to wear one of my favourite evening gowns, a daring, close-cut blue dress with a *décolleté* line which fully exposed the tops of my creamy breasts. I met Vicky Clipstone on the landing and we went down to the drawing room together where the other guests were already gathered. Sheila was already chatting happily away to Rodney Bakewell-Fisher, the ornithologist, and after Michael Harper, who was obviously Susannah's partner for the evening, had greeted us, our hostess brought over to Vicky and myself the other two gentlemen whom we had yet to meet.

The first of these was the Swiss lawyer, Oskar Gottlieb, a good-looking, slightly thickset man in his early thirties with friendly, laughing eyes who kissed my hand in the Continental manner and said: 'How delightful to meet you, Miss d'Argosse. Your face is very familiar, though I can't quite remember where we could have seen each other before. Ah, I have it, did I not see you dancing with Sir Mark Nathan at Count Gewirtz's *Quartorze Juillet* ball in Paris last year?'

I said: 'Yes, my parents and I were there, but I must confess that I don't remember us being introduced.'

He smiled roguishly and replied: 'We weren't introduced, but I could never forget such a pretty face as yours. I must confess that I tried to find out who you were, but the Count disappeared upstairs to a private room with Viscountess Allendale and Countess Marussia, and by the time he returned you were about to leave.'

'Oskar, you are incorrigible!' scolded Susannah, who had overheard our conversation. 'Take no notice of him, Rosie, Oskar can charm the birds from the trees. Now let me introduce Lieutenant Christopher Cooney to you.'

I turned round and shook hands with the handsome young soldier. He was at least five or six years younger than Oskar Gottlieb, being no more than twenty-five, clean-shaven, with a clear white skin and short straight hair. He looked very nice in his evening suit yet I must record that in my admittedly limited experience, military men rarely live up to their boasts or the expectations of their ladies. They tend to strut and brag at their clubs and in the mess, but all too often they cannot match words with deeds. Perhaps the tightness of their uniforms has something to do with it, because this is especially true of the cavalry officers, although in all fairness the boyish Lieutenant Cooney looked likely to be an exception to the rule.

Anyhow, as it happened, any interest of mine in the gallant lieutenant would have been purely academic for I could see that a bond of mutual attraction had immediately formed between him and Vicky, in the same way as Oskar had immediately appealed to me.

Indeed, Oskar and I soon found that we had an interest, that of furniture, in common and he informed me that he had spent several days in London trying to track down some genuine Chippendale chairs. [*Thomas Chippendale (1718–1779) was one of the great English master cabinet-makers of the eighteenth century – Editor*] 'There are many fine copies and it takes a good eye to distinguish true and "in-the-style-of" Chippendales. There are so many mahogany chairs with squarish backs and cabriole legs that look right until you look very closely at them,' said Oskar.

'He never stinted on the carving, though, for he had access to the best mahogany,' I remarked, taking a glass of champagne from Dennison, for my footman had been pressed into service that evening. 'His chair splats have a delicacy that often escapes the work of the copier.'

Oskar nodded his head. 'Indeed, those abroad who worked from his book would miss some of the niceties,' he agreed. 'I was recommended to a Mr Laurie in Islington who had two Chippendale-style chairs for sale and I purchased them because although not by the Master himself, they were beautifully made with interlaced ribbon backs and finely carved legs.'

We chatted away happily and Oskar escorted me into dinner whilst I noted that Sheila was taken in by Rodney Bakewell-Fisher, Vicky was on the arm of Christopher Cooney and so the ladies and gentlemen had paired up very nicely.

The repast was lavish with oysters, sole cooked in Chablis, followed (naturally) by Welsh lamb so that by the time the dessert course was due, I was feeling totally replete and I was pleased that there seemed to be a somewhat longer delay than might have been expected in the bringing in of what

I imagined would be a selection of fruits, puddings and ice creams.

Then just as I thought there may have been a problem in the kitchen, the old butler, Palmer, came in and whispered something to Michael Harper who leaned across the table and, with a wide grin on his face, asked Rodney Bakewell-Fisher if he would assist him in wheeling in the desserts trolley. 'Of course,' said the puzzled ornithologist, and he rose from the table and walked to the door, which he opened, and I could see a large table set on castors covered completely by a dazzling white cloth which reached down almost to the floor.

'Thank you, Palmer, we'll serve ourselves,' said Susannah lightly and Dennison and two maids who were acting as waitresses cleared the table and retired as Michael Harper called for silence.

'Ladies and gentlemen, we have a special surprise for one of our guests who celebrates his twenty-fourth birthday tomorrow,' he announced, and he turned to Christopher Cooney and said: 'Happy birthday, Chris, from us all, and perhaps you would now uncover this special dish which has been prepared in your honour.'

We all cheered and sang 'Happy Birthday' as Christopher got to his feet and, with a fine flourish, swept off the cloth to reveal beautifully arranged mounds of fresh hothouse fruits such as oranges, pineapples and strawberries, but the *pièce de résistance* was a living tableau in the middle of the table where, posed as still as for a photograph, were the delicious nude bodies of Jenny, my pert little chambermaid, and a dark-complexioned, shortish youth (whom I later discovered was a stable-lad on the Meverson estate). This lucky young chap was lying on his back, his skin shining from the fruit juices Jenny had rubbed onto his skin whilst Jenny herself was crouched between his legs, her lips just touching the tip of his semi-erect prick which, even as I looked, was rising perceptibly from the mass of dark curls at its root, whilst she frigged his shaft with both her hands.

At first we were too shocked to do anything but gape in silence at the erotic spectacle, but then Oskar led the well-merited applause and we watched intently as Jenny jammed down the foreskin of the youth's shaft and started to lick and lap around the purple, uncovered helmet. Simultaneously, she wriggled her glistening, naked body round so that her pussey was above the boy's mouth and then she sat down on his face and he noisily nuzzled his lips into her thatch of silky pussey hair, embedding his nose into her cunney as he flicked his tongue through her yielding love lips and, as I imagined from her grunt of contentment as she sucked his big, shiny shaft, immediately finding her clitty as he lapped her juicy honeypot.

'M'mm, what a fat young tadger, I wouldn't mind gobbling that myself,' murmured Vicky, and Susannah overheard her guest and said: 'Well, don't feel shy, darling. After all, Lewis's cock is available to any of my female guests whilst Jenny's pussey is really Christopher's birthday present.'

I turned to my left and saw that Michael Harper must have already informed the dashing cavalry officer of his good fortune, for Christopher Cooney was already tearing off his clothes and Susannah and Michael thoughtfully took the cloth which had covered Lewis and Jenny and placed it over a large Chesterfield [*a large, tightly stuffed couch upholstered in leather – Editor*].

They beckoned Christopher to the sofa and he sat there alone for just a moment, for Jenny now left off tonguing her erstwhile partner's prick to leap nimbly off the trolley and, to a roar of laughter, she padded over to the Chesterfield and plastered the best part of a jug of cream over his boner. Then she proceeded to lick it off in long, sweeping strokes whilst he lay back and groaned in ecstasy.

Even with the coating of cream, Jenny must have sensed that Christopher was in danger of spunking, because she brought her head up sharply and lay back herself to let him kiss her large, erect nipples. *Apropos* of my earlier complaint about the inability of many Englishmen to eat pussey properly, in fairness I must record that Christopher Cooney showed himself to be an exception to the rule, for he slowly kissed his way down Jenny's flat, snow-white belly to the cushion of pussey hair. I moved my chair closer and saw him lick his lips in anticipation and his tongue shot out to move slowly round her pink, pouting cunney lips and he parted them with the very tip of his tongue which sought the moist cleft where already, I was sure, Jenny's clitty was swelling. Her rounded bottom cheeks squirmed around on the cloth as Christopher sucked on her pussey and I could see the rivulets of love juice trickling down her thighs.

Jenny tossed back her head and muttered fiercely: 'Oh fuck me, sir! Please fuck me! I want your cock so much!'

This caused him to lift his head and he hauled himself over her and covered her petite frame with his broad-shouldered trunk. Jenny felt with her hand for his throbbing tool which had been sandwiched between their bellies and guided it between her thighs where it sank straight into her sopping cunt. But then, after he had begun to fuck Jenny in earnest, Christopher whispered a few words into her ear and he withdrew his prick as she hauled herself up on her knees, and they changed positions so that Christopher was now flat on his back on the wide sofa.

'What in heaven's name is he up to?' Sheila wondered with some concern in her voice, for as the youngest participant in the revels she was not as experienced as the other members of the company in the many variations of *l'art de faire l'amour*.

'Ah, well that is because Christopher went out for a long walk this afternoon and he is very probably too tired to perform in an over-energetic fashion,' explained Michael Harper, who during the evening was to prove himself a fount of wisdom on matters of an intimate nature.

'I would imagine that he has asked Jenny to do most of the work,' he went on, and in seconds was proved absolutely right as Jenny sat herself astride her partner's body. She took hold of Christopher's cock, which was waving like a flagpole in a high wind, and then lifted herself upwards over his knob and spread her cunney lips apart with her own fingers. Then she directed the tip of his knob to her gateway of delight and slowly but surely pressed herself down upon the glowing purple dome, letting him savour the glorious feeling of his shaft being enclosed by her clinging wet cunney sheath.

Christopher's hands slid under her luscious bum cheeks and Jenny wriggled around to work his iron-hard boner inside her cunt as far up as possible, and she began to bounce merrily up and down on his pulsating prick as the young officer released her buttocks to reach up and tweak her titties.

'Some men think it is demeaning to let the girl be on top, but I enjoy this lazy way of fucking occasionally,' confessed Rodney Bakewell-Fisher, and Susannah agreed with him, saying: 'I do too, sliding up and down on a nice thick prick gives the walls of my cunney a good pounding, especially if the man is well-endowed and I can grind my arse round at the same time — it gives my clitty a good rub as well.'

As she spoke, as if to prove her mistress's point, Jenny now rolled her bottom from side to side as Christopher jerked his hips, lifting himself to meet her downward thrusts. She reached between his legs and took his balls in her hand, scraping the sensitive skin with her fingernails, and Christopher began jamming his shaft upwards, so powerfully that Jenny lifted herself off him slightly, letting her pussey hover over his prancing prick as the tides of approaching orgasm overtook them. She slammed herself down again and felt the full length of his weapon twitch and contract, and then he sent a torrent of frothy spunk shooting up her love channel as she, too, climaxed and soaked his pulsing prick with her pungent cuntal juice.

'Rosie, I do hope you enjoyed that erotic show as much as I did,' remarked Oskar softly as we watched Jenny lever herself off Christopher's now softened shaft. 'It's always a pleasure to see such uninhibited fucking, is it not?'

I agreed with the sophisticated Swiss as Jenny gave Christopher's cock a final kiss before leaving the room, and he slipped on his undershorts and rejoined us at the table. After we did justice to the delectable desserts, the girls retired to the richly furnished drawing room and left the men to their vintage port and Havana cigars.

'Honestly, I do find it irritating to be excluded from the table just so the men can smoke and tell each other smutty stories,' grumbled Vicky, who like myself was an active member of Mrs Pankhurst's Women's Social and Political Union. 'After we get the vote, I think we must campaign for the reform of dinner parties!'

Susannah agreed with her and said: 'You're quite right, Vicky, why should we be treated like second-class citizens at the end of a meal? I'm sure that this silly fashion will die out in time. Meanwhile, can I offer coffee to anyone? And we must try some of this liqueur which Oskar has given to me. It is called kümmel, and he says it is very popular in Central Europe.'

She poured out tiny glasses of this drink which was new to us all. I found the delicate aroma very pleasant and Susannah added: 'Oskar says it is distilled from caraway seeds and so has a positive digestive quality as well as a delightful taste.'

After we had all downed two glasses, Vicky smacked her lips and said: 'It *is* very nice, Susannah. But I wonder if it tastes as tangy as Christopher's spunk?'

'Vicky Clipstone! You naughty girl, how could you say such a thing!' scolded Sheila, who was greatly shocked to hear her cousin speak so rudely.

'Quite easily,' said Vicky, whose tongue had been loosened by the lavish amount of wine we had all indulged in during dinner. 'I adore sucking cocks and I don't mind admitting that I'm very partial to the taste of jism, and I've always found it highly arousing when the first squirt of sticky seed shoots down my throat. What about you, Rosie?'

'Well, I must say that I like sucking cocks as well,' I said carefully. 'But perhaps more as an *hors d'oeuvres* rather than as a main course, if you follow my drift. Susannah and Sheila, what are your views on the subject?'

'Oh, I'm as keen as you are, Rosie,' replied our hostess instantly. 'I do get a thrill out of sucking a fine stiffstander but all the boys I know spend so quickly. I would prefer to suck for at least ten minutes, licking and lapping, nibbling it with my teeth and swirling my tongue over the knob. Mind sometimes I stop before the boy spends, so that his cock is rock-hard before I slip it inside my pussey.'

Sheila said timidly: 'I've only sucked Robert Bacon's cock so I don't have enough experience to offer an opinion, but although I enjoyed it, I was always slightly afraid that his prick would choke me.'

'Well, we all know about Robert Bacon of Bloomsbury, don't we, girls?' I said with a chuckle. 'And there's no doubt that he is a big boy, and I'm not surprised that you were worried about trying to cram all of his colossal cock between your lips. But with any man, so long as you remain in control, there should be no problem.

'The solution is for your man to lie still whilst you move your head. Now that way there can be no possibility of his thrusting his tool deep into your throat and making you gag — and if you're still worried, you can also grip the base of his prick in your hand to limit penetration. Then you'll find

97

you are more relaxed and you'll want to let him slide his cock in and out of your mouth for a while. However, don't feel pressured to rush things. The best way is to take your time and vary your movements and I know that you'll thoroughly enjoy bringing off your lover with your lips.'

Vicky said: 'That's good advice, Sheila, and I've just remembered that I have a little book in one of my cases which you must remind me to lend to you. It's called *Fucking For Beginners* by Dr Ian Hughes and I can recommend it to all of you.

'Now all this talk has made me feel terribly randy. Why don't we bring in the gentlemen and let's play Blind Girl's Cock.'

Susannah corrected her: 'Surely you mean Blind Man's Buff,' but Vicky's eyes gleamed as she shook her head and said: 'No, Blind Girl's Cock, it's much more fun. The game is quite simple — we bring in the four men and they undress. Then in turn I give each of their pricks a little suck before one of you blindfolds me and I finish them all off. I win a guinea for each cock I correctly identify, but I lose five guineas to each man who manages not to spunk for three minutes after I've identified his shaft.'

'Sounds fun and a good way of relieving the boys of their cash!' I remarked with a laugh. 'And I suppose one of us can take a turn afterwards, but after you've milked their pricks it would be easier for them to hold back, so we might lose our money.'

'Ah, but the second girl gets five minutes to suck them dry and, if there's a third, she gets seven minutes and so on and so on,' Vicky explained. 'However, as we were saying earlier, very few men can raise a stiffie after one sucking off, let alone two.'

'Well, this should be very interesting, but suppose the gentlemen don't want to play,' said Sheila, but Susannah, Vicky and I were quick to reassure her that this was most unlikely because none of us had ever fucked a fellow who didn't want his cock sucked. 'Men like nothing better than being gobbled,' I told her with complete confidence. 'They find it even more heavenly than we do when we have our pussies eaten. No, the boys in the dining room will be only too glad to play this lewd game.'

'Exactly so,' said Susannah as she stood up and walked to the door. 'I'll go and tell them what we have in mind and I wager they will sink their drinks, put out their cigars and be back here within ninety seconds.'

In fact, they were so eager to play that Susannah returned in under a minute and as soon as the door was closed they began undressing, throwing off their clothes until they all stood stark naked in front of us, their pricks already full and heavy-looking in anticipation of what was to come.

At Vicky's request, they stood shoulder to shoulder in a line and then she dropped to her knees and gave each of the pricks a lovely lick, lapping each cock from the tip all the way down to the balls and back up again along the sensitive underside.

By now, all four shafts were standing majestically to attention and I called out: 'Very well, gentlemen, Susannah is now going to blindfold Vicky and she will suck you off one at a time. Remember, she wins a guinea if she correctly identifies your cock, but you have a chance to win five guineas if you can hold on for three minutes after she has taken off the blindfold.'

Susannah lifted up an antimacassar from an armchair and tied the cloth round Vicky's head, turning her round to face the wall whilst I called out to the men: 'You can change places as much as you like.'

When they had settled into a line, Vicky turned round and we led her to stand immediately in front of Rodney Bakewell-Fisher. She dropped to her knees and felt for his red-domed love truncheon. She pertly stuck out her tongue and teased his knob, lazily running the tip of her pink tongue all around the edges of the springy crown whilst at the same time she manipulated his bollocks through the soft, wrinkled skin of his ballsack. Then she opened her mouth and enveloped his helmet between her lips and lustily sucked for some ten seconds on the throbbing lollipop before she pulled back her head and said! 'I'm almost certain I know who is the owner of this noble instrument.

'Yes, a little bird told me,' she giggled as she stroked his glistening shaft and we burst into applause, for of course she was referring to Rodney's ornithological interest. 'It is Rodney's prick, isn't it?'

Well, Vicky had won her guinea, but would Rodney be able to refrain from spunking in three minutes. I acted as timekeeper, using Oskar's gold hunter, and as soon as I said: 'Go!' Vicky took off her blindfold and jammed down Rodney's foreskin with her hands, bobbing her head to and fro as she sucked greedily on her meaty lollipop. Rodney's eyes were screwed up tightly and he threw back his head whilst she clasped his bum cheeks in her hands as she gobbled furiously on his pole. I could see that Rodney would be unable to last the course and sure enough before a full minute was up he spurted his frothy jism, which Vicky gulped down with evident glee. She rubbed his twitching tool in her hands until she had swallowed his complete emission and his shaft began to droop pitifully downwards.

We blindfolded Vicky again and she put out her hand, this time round the stiff, thick prick of Michael Harper. Her soft hands caressed his hairy balls as she slowly licked up and down the length of his sizeable shaft, taking her time to reach the wide, purple knob. Then she lashed her tongue around his big boner and noisily slurped away whilst her hands encircled the root and began a sliding up-and-down rhythm. This was too much for Michael to bear and before she could even guess whose cock was slewing its way in and out of her mouth, with a groan he shot a flood of hot, sticky seed down her throat.

She licked her lips as a sympathetic murmur ran round the room and the pretty girl said: 'I've never tasted this cock before but I just know that it belongs to Michael Harper.'

To a round of applause she went straight to her last task, which was to show us that she could differentiate between the two remaining pricks of Christopher and Oskar. Cleverly, she took a shaft in each hand and frigged them both and at this stage, dear reader, I realised that she could hardly go wrong for, remember, Oskar Gottlieb was of the Jewish persuasion and thus possessed the only circumcised cock on view. So once Vicky established which prick was minus its foreskin, she no longer had to guess the identity of the proud owner!

But the dear girl was nothing if not a sport and she first licked the pre-cum from the straining pink knob of Christopher's cock before gradually working his shaft inch by inch into her mouth whilst continuing to slick her left hand up and down Oskar's throbbing tool. She washed her tongue over Christopher's uncapped helmet and chirped: 'I'm glad that your fine tadger has fully recovered from its bout with Jenny,' and Christopher generously led the applause as Vicky went back to sucking his stiff prick, clasping his buttocks and squeezing him close up to her mouth until his balls were slapping against her chin.

We had no need of my timekeeping services for within seconds he shouted hoarsely: 'My God! I'm going to spend! Oh yes, that's it! I can feel my fuck juice coming! Brace yourself, Vicky!'

And with a few short, convulsive jerks of his dimpled bum cheeks, he expelled his copious emission into Vicky's willing mouth. She swallowed his jism joyfully as he quivered in convulsions of delight, sinking to his knees to join her as they wrapped their arms around each other and sealed the game with a passionate kiss.

Thus the sport ended and left poor Oskar looking very forlorn as he pulled on his clothes, but he cheered up considerably when I went across and whispered to him that I would minister to his disappointed cock later in the evening.

We spent the rest of the evening playing charades, but whilst we were being served tea before we retired to bed, Michael Harper discovered a book of verse lying underneath his chair. He showed the book to Susannah who said: 'This belongs to my Mama, she loves poetry and she must have been reading it before my parents left for London on Wednesday. Well, as you've found it, Michael, how about reading a poem to us whilst we have our tea?'

At first he demurred, but Susannah persuaded him with a kiss and after thumbing through the pages he looked up and read out:

> *When as in silks Susannah goes*
> *'Tis then methinks how sweetly flows*
> *That liquefaction of her clothes.*
>
> *Next, when I cast mine eyes and see*
> *That brave vibration each way free;*
> *O how that glittering taketh me!*

I recognised Michael's adroit adaptation of Robert Herrick's love poem, but then Christopher stepped forward to deliver some doggerel straight out of the officers' mess:

> *Oh give me a damsel of blooming sixteen,*
> *With two luscious thighs and a crack in between,*
> *With a fringe on the edge and two red lips I say,*
> *In her cunt I'd be diving by night and by day.*

So here's to the female who yields to the man,
And here's to the man who'll fuck when he can,
For fucking creates our best joys on this earth
And from fucking, you know, we all date our birth.

This lowered the level of verse and from memory Vicky recited one of the naughty limericks which are all the rage amongst the fast set:

There was a young lady of Harrow,
Who complained that her cunt was too narrow,
For times without number
She'd fuck a cucumber
But could not accomplish a marrow.

I had no objections to these naughty rhymes but I caught a glimpse of Oskar trying to stifle a yawn — after all, although his English was excellent, he was not fully conversant with the common *argot*, so I sidled over to him when Susannah adopted a Cockney accent and began:

My name is Kate, my hair is brown
And I live in a house in Kentish Town.
My pussey is smooth, not a hair in sight,
I lather and shave it every night —

Oskar smiled politely as she continued her comic monologue, but his eyes lit up when I whispered: 'Come on, let's take two glasses and the bottle of that lovely kümmel and go up to my room.'

'I would like nothing better, but wouldn't our hostess be upset if we slipped away?' he asked anxiously.

'Not in the slightest, all country house parties end with couples going off together,' I told him. 'But the usual form is to visit each other's bedrooms after lights out. However, as Susannah's aunt, who was supposed to have acted as a chaperone this weekend, is indisposed and cannot be present, we can dispense with all that hypocrisy.

'Of course you needn't come upstairs with me if you don't want to,' I added wickedly, and Oskar chuckled: 'Does a starving man refuse food, Rosie? If you would like to make your exit now, I will follow you in just a minute.'

Oskar was as good as his word and very soon afterwards we were sitting on my bed sipping this delicious liqueur. One glass led to another and in no time at all Oskar and I were travelling down a familiar road on a journey towards ecstasy – a journey that began when he tenderly took my hand in his and bestowed a burning kiss on my lips.

I returned his kiss with ardour, clasping him to me as our bodies pressed together. I moaned with delight as I felt the palm of his hand caress my bosom and my nipples hardened into hard little rubbery points against his hand. Our tongues washed against each other as with commendable dexterity he unfastened my low-cut bodice and exposed my rounded, bare breasts. His ardent lips roamed over my rosy titties, flicking them with the tip of his tongue until they stood out like two tiny red thimbles.

Now he pulled down my dress and a low, throaty growl escaped from his lips when he saw that I was wearing a garter belt, suspenders and a pair of lacy French knickers which were almost transparent. I unsnapped the belt myself, rolled down my stockings and finally wriggled out of my knickers whilst Oskar wrenched off his shirt. I unbuckled his belt and he tore off his trousers so quickly that I was concerned that he might lose a button from his flies.

My hand stole its way into the slit of his drawers and I pulled out his stiff, naked shaft which sprang out of its unwilling confinement as if on a spring, and his prick leaped and bounded between my fingers. I grasped his thick, upstanding shaft and looked with interest at his circumcised

104

cock, for it was the first time I had actually had such an organ in my hand, although I had seen the awesome member of Mr Baum, the concert pianist, at one of Lord Philip Pelham's wild gatherings in London. Therefore it was with interest that I studied Oskar's tool and I must record that I found it quite pleasing to the eye and would imagine that for the proud possessor of such a prick, it must give extra pleasure to be fucked or sucked without any additional covering over one's cock.

I tugged down his drawers and we rolled across the bed and, as our lips met in another sensuous kiss, Oskar separated my thighs and let his fingers twirl around the silky blonde hair of my pubic bush. I lay on my back as his hand continued to tease my pussey and he kissed my breasts before lowering his head between my legs. He looked up and with the lust shining from his dark, liquid eyes he declared: 'Rosie, you must have the prettiest pussey in England. It is so lovely that I will pay homage to its beauty by licking you out.'

Oskar was as good as his word and I shivered with pure bliss when he lovingly kissed my fast-moistening slit and ran his long tongue down the full length of my rolled, parted love lips. Up and down his clever tongue moved as I clasped his head between my legs and grasped at the headboard as I lost myself in the excitement of this amorous encounter.

My new Swiss lover proved himself to be one of the most adept eaters of pussey it has ever been my good fortune to meet. First, he gently parted my cunney lips with the utmost care before running his tongue very lightly along the edges of my crack, which made me almost swoon with sheer delight. I wriggled madly as Oskar quickened the pace and his tongue darted in and out of my dripping slit so quickly that I thought that I was actually being fucked! Then he found the swollen little button of my clitty and started to nip at it playfully with his teeth, rolling his tongue all around it whilst he slid two of his fingers into my open wetness.

I ran my fingers through his dark, curly hair as I felt myself getting wetter and wetter and I cried out: 'Now fuck me, Oskar, darling! I want your fat cock inside me this very instant!'

He lifted his head and in a trice he was on top of me, clutching the firm cheeks of my bottom as he guided his knob towards my tingling honeypot, and I reached down with my hands to part the pouting red love lips as Oskar manoeuvred the wide crown of his helmet between them and felt fresh flames of lust crackle through me.

'A-a-a-a-h!' he panted as he felt his shaft slide into its desired haven, and every last nerve in my entire body thrilled in exquisite rapture as I heaved up to meet his thrusts, winding my legs around him so that his heavy, hairy ballsack banged against my bum as he buried his marvellous cock in my cunt to the very hilt with deep, strong plunges that almost mashed my clitty against his pubic bone. My cuntal juices were flowing so freely that when he suddenly stopped moving and held his prick quite still inside my love channel, it sent a series of little electric shocks speeding through my trembling frame.

When my spasms stopped and I lay gasping for breath he began to stroke into me again, moving with lightning speed for perhaps a minute until I screamed out my orgasm, and only some seconds later he himself spent copiously and I gloried in the rush of liquid fire as with every throb of his quivering cock, spasm after spasm of creamy spunk, as white as liquid starch, shot into my sated pussey.

My blood was on fire as Oskar rolled off me so I slithered down the bed to kiss his pendulous balls. I kissed and sucked each one in turn and then took hold of his slippery wet length, fondling it in my hands until it stiffened up again to its former powerful solidity. Delicately, I fingered the crown of his bulbous cock and then twirled my tongue all around the ruby knob before drawing in some six inches of his majestic, velvet shaft, which seemed to grow even harder in my mouth. I sucked up and down, varying the intensity and the timing before I released the sweet tube from between my lips and looked up at Oskar's face.

His eyes were closed and he was breathing heavily as I returned to my labours and I gave his cock a long, swirling lick before plunging my lips downwards and giving the ridge around his knob a teasing little brush with my teeth. Oskar put his hands on my hips and eased me up and over him so that my dripping cunney was positioned over his face and then the dear man buried his face again in my blonde bush as he pulled me down on top of him, and I felt his tongue tracking through my pussey hair to seek out my cunney lips which were already open and welcoming, and next my clitty, engorged, erect and so sensitive to the magic touch of the tip of his tongue.

My own mouth was still busy, working its way over his knob whilst my hands cradled his lovely big balls. Soon I felt them pulsate in my palms and I guessed that he was on the verge of a climax and would be unable to hold back for much longer. Sure enough, within seconds a stream of sticky, warm seed spurted into my mouth and his prick throbbed as I held it lightly between my teeth. I sucked out all the creamy jism which poured out of his magnificent, circumcised cock and my own love juices flowed freely over Oskar's face as he gallantly continued to lap at my cunney whilst he spent.

At last I felt the spongy-testured helmet soften as I rolled my lips and nibbled away at the rounded bulb of his knob until his shaft shrivelled up into an exhausted limpness. To be absolutely honest, I was more than ready for a final fuck, but this was asking too much of Oskar — after all, the poor man had risen at six o'clock that morning to catch his train, had made the five-hour journey from London after which he had enjoyed a three-hour afternoon walk with Rodney and eaten a large dinner into the bargain.

So it was no wonder that he fell asleep in my arms. I decided to stay the night in his room and snuggled myself up against him. Although, as I say, I would have welcomed one more joust, I was far from unhappy — and, after all, there was always the morning to which I could look forward with gleeful anticipation!

CHAPTER THREE

Anyone for Tennis?

I was the first to stir after a good night's sleep and I dived down the bed to check the state of Oskar's prick. Although flaccid, it had a nice, bulky feel to it and when I rubbed my palms gently along his shaft, his turgid penis responded immediately and as soon as it had regained its full stiffness I planted a wet 'wake-up' kiss on the top of his knob.

He opened his eyes and said drowsily: 'Hello, Rosie, a very good morning to you.' Then he passed his hand over his mouth and added with a sleepy chuckle: 'I was having a wonderful dream. Some pretty girl was kissing my *schmeckle* and . . . Oh, I say, it was no dream!'

His voice trailed off as I swirled my tongue round his knob one final time and then without further ado lay back on the bed with my thighs spread widely apart. Oskar paused for a moment to admire my pouting cunney lips which protruded through my flaxen-haired pussey, and then he heaved himself over me and placed himself between my legs. With a twinkle in his dark, sensuous eyes, he took hold of his throbbing tool and cosily rubbed his knob against my crack whilst he kissed my neck and throat, and then he guided his cock between the yielding love lips directly into my cunt. I purred with pleasure as his thick tadger slid home divinely and my cunney was soon engorged by Oskar's circumcised cock. We lay still for a moment or two, enjoying the mutual sensations of repletion and possession which are so delightful to each of the participants of a loving fuck, before commencing in earnest the soul-stirring movements that would soon lead to us climbing the highest peaks of pleasure.

Oskar slowly began to move his cock backwards and forwards inside my honeypot and the feel of his hot, thick shaft squeezing its way through my wet cunney made me squeal with excited desire. My whole body started to tingle and soon I was coming off in a series of fierce little spends as he now increased the pace and pumped his prick gaily in and out of my love channel, burying his pulsating prick up to the hilt, his balls banging against my bottom. Ah, how I revelled in the joy afforded by his noble tool as it enveloped itself within the soft folds of my pussey!

'Oh God! How wonderful! Do come, Oskar! Drive on, you big-cocked boy!' I cried out as I felt the first stirrings of an exquisite climax.

Nothing loath, Oskar now fucked me in an even faster rhythm, pistoning his prick into me with swinging thrusts as my bottom arched up and down to receive his powerful strokes and we continued the fuck at a full tempo, his rampant cock plunging deeper and deeper, and my legs left the bed to wrap themselves around his back. My hands clutched at his shoulders as his body suddenly went rigid, signalling that the build-up to his spunking had already begun.

'*Gott in Himmel,*' he bellowed as his orgasm juddered to boiling point, and I felt his prick throb wildly in my honeypot as his creamy jism crashed out of his cock and coated the walls of my cunney, and my own spend came on in a rush as my saturated clitty sent waves of sheer bliss coursing through my entire body.

Dear reader, my pussey is all of a tingle at the thought of these sweet recollections of lying naked with dear Oskar on those crushed and rumpled sheets, watching the early morning sunlight and listening to the muted sounds beyond the bedroom as the Welsh countryside woke to another morn.

But there was little time to lose if we were going to take part in the lawn tennis tournament that Michael Harper had arranged for us. So I bolted back into my room and within forty-five minutes I was downstairs taking breakfast with the other guests. From the healthy, glowing cheeks of Rodney Bakewell-Fisher, I speculated that the ornithologist had spent at least part of the night in young Sheila's room, whilst Christopher Cooney and Vicky were looking adoringly into each other's eyes whilst of course Michael Harper and Susannah, our kind hostess, made little effort to conceal the fact that they were sleeping together.

'Everyone must take a hearty breakfast,' commanded Susannah gaily. 'After all, we'll need all our strength to take part in the strenuous games Michael has arranged for us this morning.'

I helped myself to some scrambled eggs, toast, marmalade and tea. 'Is that all you are having, Rosie?' asked Rodney as he sat down next to me, putting down a heaped plate of bacon, sausages, devilled kidneys and eggs.

'I was never one for a big breakfast,' I explained as he proceeded to tuck in as Oskar came and sat on my other side. He, too, was eating sparingly with just a piece of poached haddock on his plate, and I was about to comment upon this when Palmer the butler entered with an envelope on a silver salver and announced: 'Miss Susannah, a telegram has been delivered for one of your guests, Miss Rosie d'Argosse.'

My heart began to pound and the colour drained swiftly from my face — for instinctively I thought the missive would be of bad news. With trembling hands I tore open the envelope, but happily the message contained no news of illness or worse.

The telegram was from none other than my dearest friend, Lord Philip Pelham [*see 'Rosie 2: Young, Wild and Willing'* – *Editor*] and read: MUST SEE YOU. VERY URGENT. WILL BE ARRIVING AT MEVERSON HALL BY MID-AFTERNOON WITH TERENCE WHITER, PLEASE TELL SUSANNAH – PHILIP.

What could this cryptic communication mean? Susannah said that to the best of her knowledge, Philip was spending a few days in Sussex at a sporting party given by Count Gewirtz of Galicia at the large country house he rented near Broadbridge Heath. This was no surprise, for Philip was in constant demand at such gatherings for he was a first-class shot, and a bold man across country. He had a good eye for a cricket ball. Furthermore, he was a popular visitor who would amuse the women at dinner and his prick could also be relied on to perform when called upon to make some illicit nocturnal liaisons with any lonely ladies amongst the guests.

But who was Terence Whiter? I showed the telegram to Michael Harper and asked if he knew who this mysterious man might be. He thought hard for a moment and then remarked: 'It's only a guess, Rosie, but do you know Harry Whiter who owns a couple of thousand acres down in Kent? Well, I think Phil must be referring to Harry's brother, a young scamp of sixteen who, if my memory serves me right, has just been expelled from Eton.'

I thanked Michael, but his words made the whole affair even more curious. One thing was for sure, it would have to be something serious to drag Philip away from one of Count Gewirtz's lavish parties. However, all would doubtless be revealed when he arrived with young Terence Whiter. So I informed Susannah who laughed and said: 'Just like Phil, he does like to make an entrance. There are plenty of bedrooms so there's no problem accommodating them unless — but no, I simply can't believe that of Philip Pelham . . .'

'What's that?' I asked and she went on: 'He wouldn't be *involved* with this lad, would he? I mean, you say the boy was expelled from Eton, and we all know why so many young men leave public schools under a cloud. But no, whatever one has heard about Philip one has never heard a whisper of his being that way inclined!'

'Certainly not,' I said warmly. 'Let's be frank, Susannah, we've both been fucked by Philip and we are but two of his many conquests. Charming and sophisticated he may be, but Lord Philip Pelham is also a one hundred per cent, red-blooded heterosexual.'

'Yes, of course he is, how silly for the thought to even cross my mind,' said Susannah. 'I am quite ashamed of myself, but I just can't imagine why Phil should leave Count Gewirtz's shindig with a sixteen-year-old boy in tow. I can't wait to find out, I really can't!'

'Oh well, we'll all know soon enough,' said Christopher airily. 'In the meantime, don't forget that we are supposed to take part in a tennis tournament. We might not be up to Michael Harper's expertise at the game, but I for one am determined to give him a good run for his money.'

Two courts had been laid out in the gardens and the ladies were dressed in white blouses and white skirts which we wore daringly high, about six inches from the ground. My first match was against Sheila, which I lost four six, three six. My second opponent was Susannah, whom I beat six three, six two, and then I was matched against Vicky. I won the first set easily but Vicky took the second and, although we had been on court for almost an hour, we decided to play a deciding third set.

'Ready,' I called and Vicky served a rather poor shot high over the net. The ball bounced invitingly high and I drew back my arm to send back a forehand drive. Alas, perhaps through tiredness, I mistimed my return, slicing my shot badly, and the ball flew off at a tangent off the corner of my racquet at an acute angle to my right where Sheila, who had already vanquished Susannah, had been watching our match with interest. As the ball flew towards her, the sweet young girl instinctively turned her head away, but the ball thumped against her left temple and she dropped to the ground.

We rushed over to the stricken spectator and fortunately Sheila was dazed rather-than hurt. 'I'm all right,' she said, struggling to her feet. 'Do carry on, I'll just go back and take a shower before changing for luncheon.'

'Are you sure?' I asked anxiously. 'Oh, Sheila, I am so sorry.'

She smiled groggily and said: 'Don't worry, Rosie dear, it was a complete accident. I dare say you couldn't repeat that shot if you were playing for a month of Sundays.'

And she insisted that we finished the set whilst she walked slowly back through the gardens to the house. I found it hard to concentrate after this interruption and I lost the final set by two games to six.

I ran up to the net and shook hands with my conqueror. 'I think I'd better go back and make sure that Sheila is all right. Would you like to come with me?' I said to Vicky, but she declined, saying that Sheila would make a full recovery, and suggested instead that we saunter over to the other court and see how the men's tournament was progressing, although it was an academic question as to who would win, for Michael Harper had only lost one singles match in the previous eighteen months and that was in New York against the American champion, Arnold Friedlander.

So I waved goodbye to Vicky and strolled back to the house. I went straight upstairs and changed out of my tennis outfit and wrapped a silk robe round my naked body before walking across the landing to Sheila's suite. I knocked on the door and thought I heard an answer from inside so I opened the door and entered the bedroom.

There was no sign of Sheila so I called out: 'Is anyone at home?' and Sheila's shouted reply came from behind the closed door of the bathroom.

'Sheila, it's me, Rosie d'Argosse,' I said loudly as I stepped up to the bathroom door. 'I came up to see if you were feeling better.'

'Oh, thank you, Rosie, how nice of you. Do come in, the door's not locked.'

I went in and Sheila gave me a friendly wave from the large, round bathtub in which she was sitting in a pool of warm water. She said: 'There was no need for you to have come back, Rosie, I was only suffering from shock. See for yourself, the ball didn't leave a bruise.'

Leaning forward, I put my hands on her cheeks and carefully examined the pretty girl's head, thinking to myself how stunning she looked with her small but proudly jutting snowy white breasts, which were well separated with each tawny tittie looking a little away from the other, two rosebud points that were made to kiss and caress. Her belly was broad and flat, dimpled in the centre with a sweet little button and was like a smooth white plain which appeared more dazzling from the thick growth of russet pussey hair that curled in rich locks at the base between her thighs.

'No, I'm glad to say there's no sign of any mark,' I said softly and as I moved slightly to the side to check round behind her ear, one of my breasts slipped out of my robe. 'Ooh, Rosie, what big bosoms you have,' said Sheila admiringly. 'I wish mine were as big as yours.'

I looked at her slender young body and smiled as she lifted herself up out of the bath, and I spread open an enormous bath towel as I said: 'You're a very pretty girl, Sheila. I'm sure you're never short of male admirers.'

She pouted sensuously as I wrapped her up in the folds of the big towel and murmured: 'Oh, don't talk to me about men. I'm right off the male sex just at the moment.'

'Why, Sheila, you surprise me, I thought you spent the night with Rodney Bakewell-Fisher,' I exclaimed in surprise.

'I did, and he is a nice enough chap,' she answered as she snuggled herself into the towel, 'and he fucked me three times last night, but just because he is hung like a donkey Rodney thinks all he has to do is ram in his prick like a steam-hammer.'

'Oh dear,' I sighed in genuine sympathy. 'I have also come across this problem. I'm afraid that certain well-endowed gentlemen think that the mere display of their cocks send us girls into deliriums of ecstasy. Well, I'm not denying that the sight of a goodly-sized thick, stiff prick is certainly stimulating, but as the Americans say, it's not the size of the ship that counts, it's the motion of the ocean. Why, one of the best lovers I have ever entertained in my bed was a lad named Horace Bent. Poor Horace can only boast five inches at most, but he is such a considerate and imaginative partner that I always spend profusely when he fucks me.

'I never tire of telling my men that technique is far, far more important than the mere size of the instrument,' I added.

Sheila reached up and cupped my breast which was still hanging out of my robe. 'I often find that I can spend without the aid of any cock, can't you, Rosie?' she asked brazenly. 'Oh, I do hope I'm not offending you by squeezing your nice big tittie.'

'Not at all, my dear,' I replied huskily and I shucked off my robe and stood naked in front of her, and she let her hand move down and brushed her fingers through my already dampening blonde bush.

'My, your pussey's getting wet,' she giggled as she drew

her forefinger all along the length of my crack, and she clung to me whilst I rubbed her all over with the towel till she was dry, and then I dusted her gorgeous, lithe body all over with talcum powder, letting my hands linger on her breasts, bum and titties.

Then we moved to the bed and, lying naked together, we dissolved into a passionate embrace. Without further ado I spread her legs and sank my head into her fluffy little muff, flicking my tongue back and forth across her already swollen clitty. She purred with pleasure as I nibbled at the juicy morsel and gasped: 'Oh yes, how delicious. Suck my pussey, Rosie, it needs tender loving care after Rodney's big cock came crashing through it last night.

'Oooh, that's lovely,' she breathed, clutching the back of my head as I continued to lick remorselessly at her soaking slit until I felt her tremble at the approach of a climax. She writhed and twisted as her orgasm came quickly, and when it had passed I raised my head and climbed on top of her so that our two nude bodies were rubbing together cheek by jowl, or in this case, nipple to nipple and pussey to pussey.

'Now let me be the gentleman,' she whispered as she fondled my waiting breasts and swirled the hardened nipples into her mouth, sending chills of unslaked desire up and down my spine, and as her knowing fingers inched towards my cunney I felt my thighs stiffen and my hips involuntarily thrust forward in tantalising anticipation of what was to come.

Sheila traced her finger daintily through my golden pussey hair and settled on my cunt, around which she drew hard little circles until I was squirming with delight. Then, as she slid two fingers between my yielding love lips into my soaking cunney, she breathed into my ear: 'Oh, Rosie, touching you like this is making my pussey tingle. Feel my cunt, it's as wet as yours.'

117

I had not expected such passion from the demure seventeen-year-old, but with a firm hand she guided my hand between her silky, warm thighs as she kissed my titties again with unbridled lust. Then she suddenly stopped and I opened my eyes wide in shocked disappointment, but before I could say anything she murmured: 'Just lie back, darling Rosie, and I'll give you a wonderful surprise.'

What could this be, I wondered, as Sheila reached over to the bedside table and picked up an exquisite silver box which she placed on the bed between us. 'An old school friend sent me this for my birthday,' she explained as she opened the box to reveal a beautifully carved wooden two-headed dildo from Monsieur Zwaig's famous Parisian manufactory, sitting on a bed of plush purple velvet.

'This wonderful instrument has been moulded from casts taken from the magnificent pricks of His Royal Highness Prince Adrian of the Netherlands [*the consort of Countess Marussia of Samarkand and an old friend of Rosie's, whose exploits are chronicled in 'Rosie 2: Young Wild and Willing — Editor*] and Dr Jonathan Letchmore of Hertfordshire,' Sheila continued as she also took out of the box a small jar of strawberry-flavoured oil which she poured liberally over both knobs of the dildo, shaking the last drops all over my pussey.

I lay back and Sheila went to work on my cunney with her mouth, but now she added the dildo, pressing it gently to my pink love lips, using the head modelled on Prince Adrian's prick, working it in slowly but surely until it filled me as completely as the gallant Prince's prick which as readers of my earlier diaries will know, was not exactly unknown to my love channel. Then, when the godemiche was fully embedded, she lifted herself up until she was sitting astride my thighs and our eyes locked as I watched her finger herself with one hand whilst with the other she vibrated the wooden cock in my tingling cunt.

When her own pussey was ready she raised herself up and inserted the other, opposite head of the dildo into her pussey. Then she reached for me and pulled me forward until we were pressed tightly together, separated only by the stem of the splendidly carved mahogany prick.

I wrapped my arms as tightly as I could around her and Sheila wrapped hers around me and, as we rocked back and forth, we achieved a wonderful rhythm which allowed the dildo to slide thrillingly in and out of our juicy honeypots, sending pulses of sheer ecstasy to every nerve-centre in our bodies and, as our excitement grew, our fucking became even more frenzied.

'A-h-r-e, Rosie, this is divine, please don't stop!' screamed Sheila.

'I won't! I won't! How scrumptious! More! Do it more!' I gasped wildly as Sheila slid her fingers down my back with gentle, titillating strokes, sending chills of desire all along my spine whilst we continued to fuck ourselves up to the highest peaks of pleasure as this marvellous dildo prodded through our pussies, nipping its way along the grooved walls of our cunnies as we arched our bodies in absolute bliss. We fucked each other so perfectly that simultaneously we began to shudder and writhe in a veritable sea of lubricity, yelping with joy and pleasure as love juices flooded out from our cunts as we climaxed together.

We lay there quietly for some moments, our pussies still pressed together, enjoying the sensation of the dildo inside our cunts, when we were startled by a knock at the door.

'Who's there?' Sheila called out, and a continental voice replied: 'It's me, Oskar Gottlieb. May I come in?'

Sheila giggled as she looked at me and I winked back at her. 'Why not?' I said, for after all, it would be fun to see the reaction of the urbane Swiss lawyer to the sight of two naked girls lying on the bed with a double-headed dildo stuck up their noonies!

Oskar came in wearing only a dressing gown over his drawers, and how his jaw dropped when he saw Sheila and me in our happy state! However, Oskar was a true gentleman and he quickly recovered his composure and said: 'Ah, I am glad to see that you have made a complete recovery from the unfortunate accident about which Vicky informed us after Christopher and I had finished our game.'

'Did you win the match, Oskar?' I enquired, and he nodded his head absent-mindedly, for his attention was drawn to the sight of Sheila's peachy bum cheeks which she had stuck out provocatively towards him. He walked over to the bed and squatted down beside us, and when I asked him to remove the dildo, he smiled and used his long, tapering fingers to prise out the wooden knobs from our cunts.

I placed my hand on his lap and slipped my fingers through his gown to stroke his stiffening tool. 'H'mm, I suppose we should reward you for freeing us,' I said reflectively as I pulled out his prick from his drawers and started to rub my hand up and down his shaft. Sheila looked at his circumcised cock with interest and said: 'Oooh, I've never seen a dickie like this before, have you, Rosie? What's happened to your foreskin, Oskar, did you have to have it surgically removed? I hope this was not the result of catching a nasty disease!'

'No, of course he hasn't suffered from any disease, Sheila,' I said, wishing to save Oskar from any embarrassment. 'Have you never seen a circumcised cock before? All Jewish and Mohammedan boys have their foreskins chopped off in infancy.'

'Heavens, how painful!' Sheila shuddered, but Oskar chuckled as I helped to disengage his arms from his dressing-gown and replied: 'It might have been but I don't remember anything about it, being only eight days old when the operation was performed.'

I eyed his swollen phallus which was now almost at its full, majestic height before licking my lips and jamming them over his rubicund helmet whilst Sheila tugged down his drawers. 'Does it taste as good as it looks?' she enquired, and she cupped his dangling, wrinkled ballsack in her hand as she continued: 'Rosie, perhaps you would be kind enough to coat Oskar's cock with the peach-flavoured oil you'll find in the box.'

Then she turned round to present us with a close-up view of her deliciously soft rounded bottom cheeks as I placed the dildo back in its receptacle and took out the second small bottle inside the embossed silver container and, as requested, I started to pour the cool, sticky liquid over Oskar's pulsating prick.

'H'mm, how beautiful,' murmured Oskar as my fist slicked up and down his veiny shaft.

'What's so beautiful, my frigging or Sheila's bum?' I demanded, and he gave a throaty little laugh. 'Both, *mein leibchen*, though actually I was admiring that outstanding silver box,' he admitted. 'I would have to check the hallmarks but I would judge it to be English, made perhaps at the Barnard family factory about thirty years ago.'

'Well now, Oskar, my botty is also English and is only seventeen years old. Doesn't that take pride of place?' demanded Sheila as she wriggled herself up on her knees and pushed out her glorious backside towards him.

He hesitated for an instant but I pulled his thickly erect prick forward and placed it in the cleft between Sheila's bum cheeks and said: 'Do your duty, Oskar, this pretty girl wants to be bum-fucked.'

'That's right,' said Sheila, turning her face round and upwards to the surprised lawyer. 'I want a nice big pressing of juice up my arse.'

At this, Oskar went to work with a will and, parting her buttocks with his hands, jerked his hips forward so that the tip of his helmet was pushing against the puckered entrance of Sheila's rear-dimple.

'Ouch!' she ejaculated as he pushed on and soon his cock was ensconced in her tight little back passage. Soon she was responding gaily to every shove and I could see and hear Oskar's heavy balls bouncing against Sheila's bum as her buttocks were drawn irresistibly tight against his commendably flat tummy. He bottom-fucked her at a regular pace in a slowish, shunting movement, snaking his right hand round her back to let his fingers tweak her cunney, giving the girl the double pleasure of being fucked both in front and behind at the same time.

Oskar came to the boil quite quickly and with an almighty thrust he spurted his seed inside her, working his cock to and fro to warm and lubricate her back passage, though his shaft was still stiff when with an audible 'pop' he uncorked it from her well-lathered bum-hole.

I lapped up and swallowed Sheila's love juices until she climaxed and then I lay back on the bed and spread my legs open wide. Now it was Sheila's turn to grasp Oskar's cock in both hands and frig his shaft whilst she said: 'I hope you still have enough spunk in your balls to satisfy my dear friend,' as I spread open my pussey lips, revealing the glistening interior of my cunney. Oskar knelt between my thighs and aimed the knob of his throbbing tool at the mark. He began by rubbing my clitty with the tip of his cock, which made me jerk up and down quite crazily and almost took me to the brink of spending at once.

'I'm going to fuck you, Rosie,' he announced as he rolled me over onto my tummy and I felt his hand on my buttocks, parting them to let his shaft sink between them. But whilst I enjoy being taken from behind, I did not fancy a bottom-fuck so I called out: 'Don't go through the tradesmen's entrance, Oskar, I'd prefer you to proceed through the front gate.'

'Your wish is my command,' he panted and he eased his knob between the lips of my pussey and wrapped his arms around me with his hands busy squeezing and caressing my breasts. I pushed myself back onto his rigid rod as he slewed his sturdy shaft to and fro, and the quicker he pistoned his prick in and out of my juicy love-box, the wilder became my responses.

'Faster!' I yelled out shamelessly. 'Fuck me faster!' and Oskar duly obliged, quickening his pace appreciably and his prick pulsed and twitched as the honey poured from me and, as he swung forward, his prick made little sucking sounds as it entered my cunney. I thought he was going to drive on to the end of the road but instead he lay back on the bed, legs apart with his glistening wet cock raised high in the air and I sat on it, swallowing it up to the hilt inside my cunt, and I wriggled around on his sinewy shaft, dancing circles around his throbbing tool. I raised myself a little so that I kept only his knob jammed between my pussey lips which clasped his purple helmet like a mouth. My ears picked up tiny gasping sounds and I turned my head towards their source and saw Sheila standing by the side of the bed, finger-fucking herself furiously as she watched me ride Oskar's rigid rod.

Then he gripped me round the waist and pressed me down on my back again, and his circumcised shaft slicked in and out of my sopping slit as I felt my inner depths exploding into waves of pure bliss which bathed me in a truly wonderful release which flowed through every fibre of my body. I screamed with joy as Oskar's cock twitched and, with a final tremble, he shot a torrent of hot, frothy spunk inside my love channel. He pumped out his sticky libation, panting hard as my cunney milked him of the last dribbles of jism and he collapsed on top of me before rolling to one side.

Sheila stretched herself between us and Oskar turned

himself towards her and said with concern: 'You haven't spent, have you?'

'No, not yet,' she admitted. 'But it doesn't matter.'

'Oh yes it does,' he said sternly, and despite his exhaustion he heaved himself between her legs and began kissing her damp love lips. Quickly inserting his tongue between her cunney lips, he soon found her swollen clitty and simultaneously he frigged her with two fingers with his face pressed up against Sheila's crack. She writhed from side to side as he licked her out, making her scream with delight as she reached the apogee of erotic delight and a flood of love juices exploded out of her pussey which splattered over Oskar's fingers as well as his nose and lips as he sucked on her pussey and gulped down her girlish jism.

After a while Oskar and I left Sheila to dress for the picnic luncheon which Susannah's cook, Mrs Hartfield, had prepared for us in the gardens. Along with the other guests we tucked into mulligatawny soup, ragout, roast chicken, roast beef, apple dumplings and a fruit compôte.

It was almost half past two and Dennison was helping one of the maids serve coffee when we heard the familiar chug-chugging sound of a motor car being driven up the drive.

I rose from my chair and said excitedly: 'That must be Phil Pelham — I can hardly wait to find out what he meant by sending that mysterious telegram.'

Susannah and I walked back briskly to the house to greet the unexpected new guest, if indeed the car did herald the arrival of my old friend. Sure enough, as we reached the french doors of the conservatory, Palmer met us and informed us that Lord Pelham and Mr Whiter were in the hall. We hurried through and there waiting for us was the handsome scallywag himself, accompanied by a good-looking lad whom Michael Harper had speculated was the young brother of Harry Whiter, a Kentish country gentleman with whom both Susannah and I were acquainted.

'Susannah! Rosie! How lovely to see you both!' he cried, kissing us both on the cheek. 'Susannah, darling, you must forgive me for trespassing on your hospitality in this extraordinary way. I was so flustered at the time that I couldn't even find the time to use a telephone and then, in error, my man Topping sent the wire to Rosie instead of you.'

'Don't worry, Philip dear, let's get you both unpacked and then you can tell us all about it,' said Susannah with a welcoming smile as she turned to his companion. 'But first, do introduce this nice young man to us.'

'Yes, of course. Terence Whiter, meet our kind hostess, Miss Susannah Meverson, and this lady next to her is Miss Rosie d'Argosse.'

'How do you do?' said the handsome youth politely, and I could see immediately that Susannah was struck by Terence's boyish good looks. But all I was interested in was why Philip had brought the boy all the way across country from Sussex to the wilds of Pembrokeshire, probably driving through much of the night.

'You must be very tired. Come outside and have some coffee and you can meet the others,' I urged and Susannah said, 'Yes, please do, whilst I confer with Palmer about which rooms to place you in.'

So the two new arrivals followed me out to the garden and I made the necessary introductions. 'Would you two like to rest?' enquired Susannah when she came back from the house. 'Your rooms are ready.'

'That would be spiffing, Miss Meverson,' said Terence Whiter, rising to his feet. 'We only managed about three hours sleep last night in the car and I could do with some shut-eye.'

'How about you, Philip?' I asked, but he shook his head. 'No, I'd rather not, if you don't mind. I am tired but before settling down for a snooze, I'd rather like to stretch my legs for a bit as we've been cooped up in the car since we left Count Gewirtz's party yesterday.'

'I'll come for a walk with you, if you'll all excuse us,' I said promptly and Christopher called out: 'Fine, but don't be too long, Rosie, as we're starting the mixed doubles tournament at four o'clock and you and I have been drawn against Oskar and Vicky.'

I promised I would be back in good time and Philip and I strolled out through the back gate and took the track up the hill. The stone hedgebanks along the pathway were ablaze with flowers − stitchwort, foxglove and red campion − and when we reached the crest some ten minutes later we sat down on the warm grass and I said: 'Look down there at those standing stones, Phil, did you know that stones like those were transported all the way to Salisbury Plain three thousand years ago to form the inner circle of Stonehenge? And there were no roads let alone any railways to help get them there! It's a real puzzle as to how and why the stones were moved − as mysterious as the journey you and young Terence have just completed.'

Philip grinned as he rolled his jacket up into a pillow and lay his head down upon it. 'It's a strange story, Rosie, and no mistake, though if I tell you the circumstances you must promise to keep quiet about them as the tale involves the highest in the land. Honestly, it would be better if I didn't say any more about what happened at Broadbridge Heath.'

Oh-ho, I said to myself, I'll lay a pound to a penny that this involves His Majesty, the King, who was sixty-seven years old but still, according to London gossip, very active between the sheets with Mrs Keppel and, when in France, with a variety of saucy chorus girls.

'Come on, Phil, I won't spill the beans,' I coaxed, curling myself up to him. 'You know I can keep a secret.'

My old friend sighed and then gave a little chuckle. 'Yes,

I know you can, Rosie. What the heck, why should I deprive you of a good laugh?'

And then he proceeded to relate what had happened at Count Gewirtz's get-together, and the only reason that I am recounting the tale is that later His Majesty saw the funny side of the incident and repeated it to Mrs Greville at a sporting weekend only a few weeks later, although of course it is still hardly common knowledge.

Philip and I settled down and he began: 'Well, we all arrived in good time for luncheon on Wednesday afternoon and, knowing His Majesty's fondness for good food, Count Gewirtz had engaged the famed Mrs Bickler as cook for the four days he planned to stay at Allendale Priory, the country mansion he had rented from Colonel Horrocks. So, as you may imagine, every meal was a feast and that first luncheon was more of a banquet designed especially for the King. We had poussin stuffed with quails' eggs, fillet of lemon sole, a splendid sirloin of beef, a cream pudding, a savoury and cheeses all accompanied by the very finest of clarets and champagne from Colonel Horrocks's extensive cellars.

'After luncheon, I asked young Terence if he would care to accompany me for a constitutional for I needed to walk off the substantial meal we had consumed. He gratefully accepted, for I am sure he had not really wanted to come, but his parents, Sir Roger and Lady Elizabeth Whiter, had insisted that he joined them, for they were not prepared to leave him to his own devices after his unfortunate exit from Eton College. I should add here that Sir Roger and Lady Elizabeth Whiter themselves had been invited to Allendale Priory by the Count on the express wish of the King, who I am sure was keen on a midnight dalliance with Lady Elizabeth.

'Anyhow, Terence and I sauntered down past the croquet lawn and through the orchard and I carried a bag of pastries which Johnny Gewirtz had insisted we take with us in case we fancied an early tea-time snack. As we strolled along I said to Terence that it was rotten luck having to spend four days here with no-one of his own age to keep him company. "It must be very boring for you," I said to him with genuine sympathy.

' "Yes, it's not been a good year for me," answered Terence as he moodily kicked at a pebble on the path. "I suppose you know that I was chucked out of Eton earlier this year?"

' "Yes, I had heard about that unfortunate incident, old chap," I replied consolingly. "May I ask why, or perhaps this is a matter you would prefer not to discuss?"

' "No, I don't mind talking about it, Lord Philip, for I still don't believe that I did anything terribly wrong. It all began one afternoon when I had just come into my study after a grand game of footer, feeling very pleased with life in general, for we had just beaten Charterhouse by three goals to two and I had scored the winner three minutes from time. I had showered with the fellows in the changing room and when I looked in the mirror in my study, I could see my cheeks were glowing and as I said, I was feeling on top of the world. Perhaps it was this very sense of well-being that caused my prick to suddenly begin to swell, as I had not been thinking any sensual thoughts whatsoever, but my member often springs to life as if it had a will of its own."

' "Don't worry, this happens to all young men," I advised him and he nodded. "Thank you, but I did know this could be expected because my Uncle Edmund had given me a copy of Dr Billy Bucknall's *Human Sexuality Explained For Young People* for my sixteenth birthday. I tried to adjust my trousers but my cock simply would not go down, so I lightly stroked my shaft until there was a sudden cough behind me and I whirled round to see Patricia, one of the housemaids, behind me. 'I've come to do your bed, Master

128

Terence,' she said with a leer. 'Though from the look of you I'm sure that's not the only thing I could do for you.'

' "I blushed and the bold girl moved forward and muttered: 'I can see your tadger trying to poke its way out of your trousers, the poor thing. Why don't we put it out of its misery?' And with that she came over to where I was standing, knelt down in front of me and, after unbuckling my belt, began to undo my fly buttons! When she pulled down my trousers and pants, my cock sprang up to greet her and I almost fainted with delight when she took my prick in her soft, warm hands. No girl had ever tossed me off before and I thought I was going to come then and there when she said: 'Aren't you well-developed, Master Terence! My, what a thick cock you've got for a boy of sixteen. I'll bet it's the biggest in the whole of the Upper Fifth.'

' "As it happened, she was quite correct and false modesty not being one of my vices, I told her so. She smiled as with one hand she continued to rub her hand up and down my stiffie and with the other she swiftly undid the buttons of her blouse and uncovered her breasts for me to see. I'd only seen photographs of bare breasts in a copy of *Cremorne* which Bolsover Major smuggled in during the previous term, but here in front of my eyes were two gorgeous, snowy white globes topped with cherry-red nipples. I could scarcely believe my eyes as she tweaked her titties with the tip of my knob and I let out a hoarse little cry of delight.

' " 'Do you like that, Master Terence?' Patricia whispered with a gleam in her eye, and all I could do was nod my head as I was far too excited to reply coherently.

' " 'Well, if you like that, see what you think of this,' she hissed, and to my astonishment she took my prick between her lips and began sucking my cock, teasing my knob against the roof of her mouth. Her darting tongue washed all round my helmet and I thrust my quivering prick forward as her hot, wet tongue lashed against my throbbing tool. The exquisite washing of her tongue on my shaft caused me to come almost straight away and she sensed this and let go of my twitching tool for a brief moment. Then she returned to the attack, licking the underside and squeezing her hand around the base of my cock whilst she licked and lapped so wonderfully that I simply could not prolong this delicious feeling any longer.

' "I'm coming," I gasped and as the spunk rushed up from my balls, she clamped her lips round my cock and sucked away lustily, and in seconds I had flooded her mouth out with my sticky seed. My jism filled her mouth and gushed out from her lips and after she had gulped down my foamy emission, she smacked her lips and said: 'Goodness me, not only have you got the largest cock in Eton but I've never known any boy spunk like that. I was nearly drowning in it!'

' "Oh, I'm sorry, I didn't mean to make you swallow my cum," I said falteringly, but she laughed and said: 'Don't apologise, my dear. I love the taste of spunk, it's nicer than almost anything I know. Do you know that your form master, Mr Cowen, once told me that there was an Empress of Russia called Catherine the Great who used to suck off three men every morning before breakfast because she liked the taste so much!'

' "You've sucked Mr Cowen's cock?" I gasped in astonishment and she nodded gaily and replied: 'Oh, yes, Jimmy's a game old boy and enjoys nothing better than a good sucking off.'

' "I could hardly believe my ears, but Patricia gave me a quick kiss and said she had to go, saying: 'I'll come back here at this time on Thursday, and then you can fuck me if you like. You've never fucked a girl before, have you? You'll love it, Master Terence, it's great fun!' "

' "You lucky young pup," I said enviously to young Terence. "I would have given everything I had for an

130

afternoon with a girl like Patricia when I was your age.''

'He shrugged his shoulders and said nothing for a while as we decided not to continue our walk because it was now very warm, so we turned round and began to tramp back to the house. Then Terence said: ''What happened next was most unfortunate. After lights out in the dormitory, I could not sleep for thinking about Patricia's bare white breasts with their jutting strawberry titties and I let myself drool about how I would let my hands rove across those soft spheres and then down to her curly bush where her pouting pussey would be waiting for my sturdy shaft.

' ''Naturally, these lewd thoughts made my prick swell up to a capital stiffstander and when I judged that everyone else was asleep, I began to give myself some much-needed relief, capping and uncapping the bulging red helmet in my fist. I was so engrossed in this erotic reverie that I did not even see the door open and Patricia steal in and stand by my bed, dressed only in a light robe.

' '' 'Oooh, have you started without me, you naughty boy?' she hissed as she slid out of her robe and slipped into my bed and added: 'I don't see why we should wait till Thursday for our fuck.'

' '' 'Neither do I,' I whispered back and our naked bodies pressed together as our lips met in a lusty wet kiss. Patricia turned sideways so that I could insert my hand between her legs and explore her pussey which was thatched with a light covering of curly hair. 'Kiss my titties, Terry, they love being suckled,' she panted and I wasted no time licking and nipping those jutting rubbery strawberries and then, just as she grasped hold of my throbbing cock, disaster struck.''

' ''What happened?'' I asked and Terence grimaced: ''I was just about to roll on top of her and plunge my prick in her waiting pussey when the door of the dorm opened and Mr Cowen came in to make sure we were all in our own beds. It was not regarded as such a great crime if you were

131

found having a mutual wank and the standard punishment was a short lecture and six of the best, on your bum. But because I was found in bed with a girl instead of another boy, I was expelled for gross misbehaviour! And of course Patricia was also dismissed the very next morning. Luckily, though, I telephoned my Aunt Gwendolen who I knew had a vacancy for a willing parlourmaid and on my recommendation she engaged Patricia there and then, so at least the poor girl didn't find herself penniless on the streets."

'We were now in sight of the house and Terence went on: "Although my parents were very angry with me, and I now have to work very hard for my Oxford University examinations with a private tutor at home, at least I can look forward to my next visit to London and take tea with Auntie Gwen in Bedford Square!

' "I say, I think I have a photograph of Patricia she sent me the other day — would you like to see it, Phil?"

' "Very much so," I said, adding: "If Patricia has a friend of a similar nature, perhaps we could make up a foursome and take the girls out on their day off — and I don't have any tenants in my town house this year, so we could have some real fun together!"

' "That would be jolly," said Terence as we walked into the house and went upstairs to his bedroom, where he rummaged in his case for a photograph of his beloved. Meanwhile, I took out the pastries that Mrs Bickler had given me and put them on a plate by the open window. Terence found the photograph, but as he handed it to me we heard the sound of a high-pitched squawk followed by a burst of girlish giggling float up from below. We craned our heads out of the window and saw none other than His Majesty with Lady Chigleigh who was wagging her finger at the grinning monarch.

' "Oooh, you naughty King," she squealed in mock

anger. "Can't a lady bend down to pluck a flower without having her bottom assaulted. How would you like it if I pinched your cock, sire?"

' "I would have no objection whatsoever, m'dear," he rejoined, taking her hand in his own and planting it directly upon the royal rod, and the lusty Lady Sheena Chigleigh giggled saucily as the King cupped the firm swell of her proud young bosoms in his hands before pulling open her blouse to uncover her bare breasts.

' "That's nice, very nice indeed," she purred as he tweaked her titties between his fingers, and she swiftly unbuttoned his trousers and took out the royal cock, and her silky stroking soon had his sizeable shaft hard and erect as it twitched in her grip.

'With a throaty growl the King ripped off her blouse along with his jacket and began to pull down her skirt, but she wriggled out of his grasp and said: "We can't fuck here, sire, not out in the open air."

' "Kings can do as they please, Sheena," he retorted warmly. "And anyhow, there's no-one about, everyone else has gone off bicycling down to Southwater — except for Phil Pelham and young Terence Whiter who are out walking and our genial host, Johnny Gewirtz, who informed me at luncheon that he planned to spend the afternoon fucking Miss Rosamund Fortescue. Still, if you prefer the privacy of the bedroom, so be it. But at least suck me off before we go indoors."

' "It will be my pleasure," she cooed and dropped to her knees, opening her mouth wide, she slipped in his bulbous knob whilst sliding her fist up and down his thick, gnarled shaft. Terence leaned forward to obtain a better view but his sleeve caught the plate of pastries and sent it toppling out of the window. Fortunately, the plate only caught the King a glancing blow on the shoulder, but two of the pastries landed smack on top of His Majesty's head and an angry bellow of rage escaped from his lips as Terence and I both pulled back immediately from the window.

' "Oh crumbs, that's torn it," gasped Terence, his face as white as a sheet. I popped my head out again quickly and saw the King dancing wildly about, howling with wrath and clawing at a sticky mess of jam and cream which was plastered over his head and shoulders. "Quick now, Terence, we'd better make ourselves scarce," I said to him and we rushed out onto the landing and ran upstairs to the billiards room.'

Philip paused for breath and I chuckled as I made myself more comfortable as I laid my head inside the crook of his shoulder. 'What a hoot,' I said. 'Still, you weren't caught so I don't quite understand why you had to leave the gathering in disgrace.'

'Fair comment, my love,' he grunted as I cuddled up to him. 'The trouble was that Lady Sheena had been so startled when the plate come whizzing down that she closed her teeth far too sharply round the King's shaft and the scream we heard was one of agony rather than anger.

'Well, to cut a long story short, Count Gewirtz insisted on calling in a doctor, who we knew would be sworn to silence by virtue of his Hippocratic oath and thankfully, although the royal prick was painfully sore, the doctor pronounced it undamaged. However, Lady Sheena was now in such disgrace that Terence and I felt it necessary to shoulder the blame and later that evening we confessed our guilt, stressing of course the purely accidental character of the incident. I expected an explosion for His Majesty has been short-tempered of late, but he simply glowered at us and muttered: "The whole affair is best forgotten," and he marched out of the room without saying another word, slamming the door shut behind him.

'But Johnny Gewirtz, whom I had asked to be present during this painful conversation, asked us to wait on and said to us: "Philip, I would strongly advise you and this young man to leave the house first thing tomorrow morning. Incidents like this somehow soon find their way into scurrilous gossip and the wisest course of action for you and Terence is to take a holiday abroad for at least a week or two, somewhere far from the madding crowd where you will not be questioned. Furthermore, I suggest that you travel separately, to avoid any possible identification.

' "Terence, I have an errand you could perform for me. I need someone to take some papers to a business associate of mine in Rome. If you would care to undertake this task, I will pay all expenses for yourself and a slightly older person to go to Rome, and I'll also give you fifty pounds for your trouble. I will speak to your parents and tell them how such a visit would be most educational. If you leave before breakfast, of course, it will be a *fait accompli*, but I am sure I can talk them round.

' "Now how about you, Philip? Will you heed my advice?"

'I nodded miserably, for I trusted the judgement of the sophisticated Count Gewirtz who was a true and trusted friend. "I'll book myself a passage to Barcelona. Your agent in Catalonia, Senor Ribalta, wrote to me only last month that I should find time to visit him this summer. Do you need any documents to be taken out to him?"

'He declined my offer with thanks and well, that's it, Rosie. I'm travelling back to London tomorrow and then on to Spain.'

Philip finished with a sigh and I mulled over his long tale. 'I'm sorry to hear that you've had such troubles, but all will be well,' I said with as much reassurance as I could muster. 'A trip abroad can be such fun. Gosh, I really envy Terence his task because Italy is my favourite country, and I would love to have taken the Count's papers over for him.'

'Would you really, Rosie? To be honest, I decided to come

here to see you because it's so far out in the wilds and also because I wondered if you could suggest any fellow of about our age who might like to go to Rome with young Terence.'

I shook my head but then I had an idea. 'Can't I go with him, Phil? If I can persuade my Papa, I'm sure he'll agree for he's in the Foreign Office and if you tell him, which you can in all honesty, that my journey is to be kept secret as it involves a very sensitive matter, I'm sure he won't object — especially if you tell him that Count Gewirtz will back your request.'

He stared at me and said: 'Are you joking, Rosie?'

'No, honestly, I'm not,' I said firmly, tapping him on the nose. 'We don't have a telephone here but Susannah mentioned in our letters of invitation that in an emergency we could motor down to Cardigan and use the Post Office telegraph there. Do it this afternoon — you've plenty of time, the Post Office doesn't close till six o'clock. My parents are away, incidentally, so you must send the wire to the Caledonian Hotel in Edinburgh.'

Poor Philip could hardly believe it but when he finally saw that I was in earnest, he gave a short laugh and said: 'Well, one thing's for sure. Young Terence will be delighted as he's one of your secret admirers! When I told him that you would be here he said: "Will I really meet Miss d'Argosse? I've seen her photograph in the papers and she is the prettiest girl I've ever seen." '

'Oh stop it, Philip,' I chuckled as he squeezed me even closer to him. 'You're making that up.'

'I promise you that I'm not,' he protested, his merry blue eyes now sparkling with bright mischief and, as ever, the sensual energy that he generated was beginning to affect me. I was helpless as Philip mentally undressed me with his usual panache which, whilst making me feel naked under his gaze, in no way offended me.

'Would you care to be fucked, Rosie?' he enquired with

the utmost tenderness in his voice, 'as I'm off to Spain tomorrow and you may be on your way to Rome, heaven knows when we'll have another chance to make love.'

'What a splendid idea, Phil, I thought you'd never ask!' I replied and lay back to enjoy the sweetest of kisses whilst he unbuttoned my blouse and started to caress my breasts. As we embraced I felt his noble cock stiffen against my tummy as I kicked off my shoes and helped Philip take off the rest of my clothes until I was naked. Then he shrugged off his own garments, spreading out his shirt so we could lie upon it, and I slid my hand across his manly chest and then lowered my wrist until I had his rock-hard swollen shaft in my fist. How stiff and hot it was in my grasp and I let out a tiny 'wow!' as Philip reciprocated by dipping his own hand between my thighs, running his fingertips through my silky muff of golden pussey hair, and then he gently penetrated my cunney with his forefinger and my honeypot began to moisten under his experienced touch.

The soft light made the ripples of Philip's body glow and I could hardly wait for him to fill me with his thick prick as the musky aroma of maleness filled my nostrils. He kissed me passionately, starting on my neck and throat before moving down to my high-tipped breasts. His full lips enveloped my engorged red nipples and he sucked hungrily upon them as his tongue teased the erect rubbery titties, making me quiver all over with carnal excitement. Then I pulled his head down to my fluffy bush and he licked and lapped at my tingling pussey, his tongue sliding through a smooth passageway between my love lips to wash around my pulsating clitty.

'Oooh, oooh, oooh!' I moaned as I climaxed delightfully, whilst he continued to kiss and suck my sopping slit until he raised himself on his knees and took his throbbing tadger in his hand. He gave it a quick rub and then without further ado he pushed the rounded helmet against my yielding pussey lips which opened like magic to receive him. How I relished the feel of Philip's broad boner inside my love-box! He began to thrust hard and fast, his wrinkled pink ballsack slapping my bum cheeks as he swung his cock in and out of my cunt whilst his hands played with my breasts.

Oh, how we enjoyed this passionate fuck on the brow of that Welsh hill that warm midsummer afternoon! I will never forget how with every thrust of his superb shaft my own hips thrust back, kissing his cock with all the muscles of my cunney. We rocked to and fro as I waggled my bum to obtain every inch of his marvellous member inside me and I shuddered with delight as its fat, gleaming head stretched my cunt which had somehow expanded to receive his pulsating organ.

Again and again he pounded his prick into my pussey, faster and faster at a tremendous rate of knots which I could no longer even attempt to match. Oh how I loved each powerful stroke as my cuntal juices coated his cock, making it slide in and out even more freely.

'God, I'm going to spend again!' I yelled out as my moment of truth rapidly approached. 'Shoot your spunk, Phil, fill my cunt with your creamy jism, you lovely fucker!'

His slim body went rigid and his face contorted as his own orgasm was also very near. He cried out hoarsely as he shot a thrilling torrent of gushing seed into my crack before his body relaxed and he pressed his lithe frame slowly down on top of me, careful to keep his cock inside my cunney as we calmed down.

'Alpha plus, my lord, that was truly magnificent,' I said, kissing him on the lips. 'As they say in America, you fuck like a rattlesnake.'

'Thank you, Rosie, we always have a good time together, don't we?' he said, rising up to pull on his drawers. 'Alas, I wish we had more time but I must go to Cardigan and send the telegram to your Papa, and I dare say you had better rejoin the others on the tennis courts or they might send out a search party for you!'

So we dressed ourselves and sauntered back to Meverson Hall. I changed back into a tennis dress and waved goodbye to Philip as he made his way to the motor house.

When I arrived at the tennis courts, a game of mixed doubles was taking place between Sheila and Christopher against Susannah and Michael. 'What's the score?' I asked Oskar, who was the sole spectator. 'And come to think of it, where have Vicky and Rodney disappeared to? I hope you haven't been waiting for me to show up.'

'No, not at all, I've only been here for five minutes myself, and the last I saw of Vicky and Rodney they were disappearing into Rodney's bedroom after luncheon,' said Oskar as he applauded Christopher's athleticism in reaching a surprisingly fast serve from Susannah which hit the ground in front of him and broke sharply to the right. It looked a winner but the cavalry officer caught the ball with a superb half volley and lifted it low across the net.

'Well played, sir!' I called out and Christopher acknowledged my applause with a wave of his racquet. Oskar and I sat down to watch a thrilling game, for although Michael Harper was far and away the most talented player on court, Susannah was probably the weakest and this evened up the contest to give Christopher and Sheila a fighting chance to steal some points. When Michael served, retreat to the back line was the only possible recourse, but both Christopher and Sheila managed to return Susannah's serves with comparative ease. Every game was hotly contested and every point was fought for but in the end, after almost three quarters of an hour, Michael and Susannah finally triumphed by six games to four.

With perfect timing, Palmer, Dennison and my pert little chambermaid, Jenny, now arrived on the scene trundling tea trolleys in front of them and they were soon followed by Vicky and Rodney whose flushed faces betrayed the fact that they had been engaging in some strenuous indoor exercises!

I first sat down next to Susannah and told her that I would have to leave Meverson Hall in the morning. I begged her to excuse my early departure and said that although I was not at liberty at this time to clarify the circumstances to her, I had been asked to assist Philip Pelham resolve a delicate situation and that it would be churlish to refuse him.

'I quite understand, Rosie,' said Susannah scratching her head in puzzlement. 'Well, actually I don't, but I'm sure it must be a very important affair because you were enjoying yourself here, weren't you?'

'When the matter is finally resolved, I'll be happy to explain everything in full detail,' I promised, and happily this satisfied Susannah who gave orders to Jenny to help me pack my cases this evening, and to Palmer to have Owen the chauffeur on call early tomorrow morning with the Mercedes in good time to transport me to Carmarthen Station.

After tea I had a quick word with Dennison and instructed him to be ready to leave tomorrow morning, and then I played what was to be my final game of tennis — a hard-fought doubles match with Oskar against Rodney and Vicky which we won by six games to three. Oskar and Rodney stayed on court to be coached on the finer points of the game by Michael, but Vicky and I decided to call it a day and sauntered back to the house.

'You must be very fit, Rosie, as you were scampering around the court during our game, even though you'd been playing tennis all afternoon whilst I was fagged by the middle of the set,' said Vicky as we reached the open French doors to the lounge.

'Not really, in fact I was only watching the others before

you came, as I'd been canoodling with Lord Pelham till nearly half past three,' I confessed.

Her face brightened as we sank ourselves into two comfortable armchairs and she went on: 'Oh, so then I wasn't the only one to enjoy a post-prandial fuck, though poor Rodney needed some extra help to get a cock-stand after our first joust.'

Her words added weight to my long-held argument that the prick is the most treacherous of all the male organs. So often, and at times without any reasonable cause, it wilfully insists on countermanding the orders of its owner. And I do not refer just to its disloyal refusal to do its duty in bed but also to its contrary habit of erecting itself at the wrong time and in the wrong place. Many young men in particular are afflicted by this strange contrariness, being embarrassed by a sudden bulge in their trousers in a public place, only to find their weapons flaccidly uncocked whilst spooning with the object of their affections just a few hours later!

So it was with interest that I urged Vicky to tell me more about poor Rodney's recalcitrant rod and she was happy to comply, saying: 'I knew that Rodney was keen on some rumpy-pumpy because although during luncheon he was across the table from me and had no opportunity to say so directly, he sent me unmistakable messages under the tablecloth. He had taken off his right shoe and during the meal he was busy rubbing his toes up and down my legs. I said nothing but slipped off my own shoes and reciprocated so that he would know that his attentions were not unwelcome.

'So after luncheon we quietly left you all down here and went upstairs to Rodney's bedroom. We wasted little time in preliminaries and after a passionate embrace, I said to Rodney: "Let's take off all our clothes now so as not to get them crumpled." So we undressed and I carefully hung my dress on a hanger and carefully folded my underclothes in a neat pile. I turned round to see that Rodney had already stripped off and was standing naked in front of me, his cock standing up high and mighty as we engaged in a delicious wet kiss, our tongues flicking away in each other's mouths and our hands running all over each other's bodies as we staggered to the bed and lay entwined upon the eiderdown.

'I grasped his hard cock and slid my hand up and down the hot, stiff shaft, but to my distress his prick began to twitch wildly in my hand and before we had really even started to enjoy ourselves, he groaned and he discharged a sticky fountain of jism all over my fingers.'

'Oh dear, so Rodney suffers from a hair-trigger,' I commented and Vicky sighed and said: 'I thought he was just over-excited but let me first finish telling you what happened.

'I gave his cock a little kiss and said cheerfully: "Don't worry, Rodney, I'll soon make you splendid again." I slid out of bed and stood in front of him and then opened my legs wide and began to stroke my moist pussey through my curly bush. I slipped my finger inside my slit and began to frig myself as he looked on with wide-eyed interest. I was sure this would do the trick but his prick obstinately refused to rise up except for a slight thickening of the shaft. So I tried licking and sucking his soft staff, tonguing his knob whilst his hands played laconically in my hair, but this, too, failed to produce any response.

'Rodney cleared his throat and said: "Um, I must apologise for my silly refusal to play the game. I'm a very naughty boy and richly deserve to be punished. Vicky, would you please chastise me? I need a good spanking."

'He rolled over onto his tummy and stuck his bum in the air. "Are you sure this is what you want?" I asked and he replied in a small voice: "Slap one cheek at a time," so I straddled his legs and prepared to administer the punishment. He wasn't the first man I've met who needed a whacking before being able to fuck, and I'm sure you have come across the same phenomenon.'

'*Le vice anglais*, I said, shaking my head thoughtfully. 'Dr Letchmore once took me to a lecture by the noted Professor Hammond who propounded the theory that the anxiety and guilt drummed into young boys at school has much to do with this matter.'

'The public schools certainly have much to answer for,' she agreed and went on: 'Anyway, I did what he asked and began to spank him, laying the slaps only on the right cheek of his bum, not touching the left one at all. "Ow, Ow, Ow!" he cried out as the smacks sounded loudly as they fell in slow succession on his plump, firm backside. After a dozen smart slaps I inspected his bottom which looked rather odd with the bright scarlet colour of the spanked cheek contrasting strongly with the snow-like whiteness of the untouched buttock. So I set to work on the virgin cheek and he winced and wriggled his bum the whole time whilst I gave him twelve sharp smacks.

'Now his posterior was red all over but my face fell as he hauled himself on to his side and I saw that his prick was still at best only semi-erect. "Well, what now, Rodney?" I asked in desperation and in reply he opened his bedside table and took out − '

'Not a dildo, surely,' I interrupted, thinking back to the double-headed godemiche that her cousin Sheila had produced during our all-girl romp before luncheon.

'Well, yes, in a manner of speaking,' said Vicky, who no doubt wondered how I could have guessed what she was about to say. 'Not one of the wonderful ladies' comforters like those produced by Monsieur Zwaig of Paris, but a long, rather thin affair coloured pink and shaped more like a candle than a cock. He anointed it with some oil from a tiny bottle and I rolled onto my back, thinking that he was going to finish me off with it — but I was wrong.

'Instead, he gave me the instrument and he scrambled onto his knees and pulled apart his still smarting bum cheeks. "Shove this up my arse, Vicky, and you'll see how quickly I'll get a capital stiffstander," he muttered.

'This was a new game to me, Rosie, but I'll try almost anything once, so I grasped the imitation member as Rodney raised his knees and pulled them back till they touched his chest, and his nether region was now completely exposed to me. Gingerly, I took hold of his limp shaft and looked underneath his dangling ballsack where his wrinkled little arsehole was staring up at me whilst Rodney panted: "Yes, go on, dear girl, gently does it."

'I placed the tip of the dildo against the tiny puckered entrance and pressed it lightly inwards and the slippery mock phallus slipped a full inch into its tight sheath. Frankly, I found the experience somewhat unnerving but Rodney didn't seem to be too uncomfortable.

' "Aaah! That's just the ticket, Vicky," he grunted hoarsely and as I pressed forward another few inches Rodney groaned and quite suddenly his orifice relaxed and I inserted fully half the candle up his bum.

' "Now fuck me with it," he commanded and so I pulled the greasy pole out a couple of inches, before pushing it back up again. "Yow-ow-ow!" hissed Rodney through clenched teeth as I drove the dildo in and out, rotating it in small tight circles as he grabbed his own cock and began to frig himself vigorously and, to my delight, his prick was now rampant, its mushroom uncapped helmet standing proudly on top of a thick, pulsing shaft.

'I was in no mood to waste this fine erection so I hastily clambered up on top of him and guided his knob between my pouting pussey lips and I bounced up and down on his juicy cock as I continued to hold the dildo steady whilst

144

Rodney fucked himself on it with powerful, thrusting hip movements, levering himself up and down exactly as I was doing on his own throbbing tool. With my free hand I reached down to my sopping cunt and lightly flicked at my clitty which was by now popping out from between my love lips.

'We were now both so fired up that my cuntal juices began to flow and Rodney grabbed my bum cheeks in his hands as he gloried in the sensations of fucking and being fucked at the same time. He came with a huge rush of frothy jism which flooded my cunney and I went off shortly afterwards so all was well. But isn't it quite weird what has to be done to coax some cocks to stand up and be counted!'

'How very true! But tell me, has Rodney any idea what has caused this strange pattern of behaviour?'

Vicky spread out her hands and said: 'Oh yes, his story fits in with your earlier comment. It seems that when Rodney was in the second form at St Birchemalls, there was one sadistic master who used to frig the boys whilst he caned them and he also suffered at the hands of the captain of cricket who used to bugger the prettier boys whenever he had the chance.'

As I mulled over her answer, we heard the unmistakable noise of Philip's car drawing up and I excused myself and ran out to greet him. He climbed out of the car as I approached and gave the thumbs-up sign. 'Good news, Rosie, I sent a wire using a special code word used by the Foreign Office to denote an emergency. Go back to the Savoy Hotel in London and I'll wager a thousand pounds that you'll have a telegram delivered to you from your Papa giving you his blessing to spend ten days in Rome with Count Gewirtz's associate, Signor Carlo Nettlotone. Now, has young Terence woken up yet? We must hurry and give him the good news.'

Dear reader, I can hardly find the words to describe the excitement! I thought of the words of Dr Johnson who once declaimed that a man who has not been to Italy is always conscious of an inferiority. We rushed up to tell Terence about all the arrangements, and after dinner I retired early for we had to leave Meverson Hall early to make the necessary connections for the London express. Nevertheless, Philip came to my room at half past ten and I need hardly record how we spent the next three hours!

CHAPTER FOUR

Roman Scandals

For the sake of brevity I will just briefly sketch the details of how, just a little more than four days after returning to London, I came to be sitting in the cool, marble-floored drawing room of Carlo Nettolone's beautiful villa off the Via Tiburtina on the outskirts of the Eternal City.

As Lord Philip Pelham had correctly surmised, my father readily gave his approval for my new trip. Philip made all the travel arrangements at breakneck speed via the excellent offices of Thomas Cook and the following afternoon, he and Dennison (who returned home to Argosse Towers) saw Terence Whiter and myself off at Victoria Station. Although all this hectic travelling was very tiring, young Terence proved himself an amiable companion and we were able to rest in comfort on the luxurious Blue Train which, whilst we slept, sped us through France all the way to Genoa.

There we changed trains for Rome and here I must relate an incident that took place as we journeyed in our private compartment on the Milan to Rome express. I was reading a copy of *The Times* I had purchased at the station bookstall in Milan and Terence was gazing out of the window at the rolling Tuscan hills.

'I can hardly believe what has happened to me over the last few days,' said the handsome youth with a small, pensive sigh. 'Do you know, now and then I've been pinching myself to see if I'll wake up and find out that all this is merely an amazing dream.'

Putting down my newspaper I looked hard at the lad, whose head must be whirling after all that had happened to him since the fateful moment when he sent a plate of cream cakes crashing down upon the portly figure of His Royal Majesty King Edward VII. 'This is no dream, though I am sure that you must be rather homesick,' I assured him kindly. 'But don't worry, all being well, we'll be back in England within a month.'

'Oh, I'm not homesick at all,' he replied robustly. 'This is all great fun and far better than cramming for my exams with my tutor.'

'You must be fed up with all these train journeys, though,' I said. 'I know that I feel that I've been living for the last week in a railway carriage and I can't wait to get to Rome.'

Terence shrugged his shoulders. 'Railway journeys don't bother me at all. In fact I really enjoy travelling by train far more than by horse or motor car. I must have inherited this attribute from my great-great-uncle, Major Terence Whetstone, one of the first pioneers of the steam engine. I was named after him, as a matter of fact.'

'How interesting, Terence. Was your uncle a friend of George Stephenson?'

'Absolutely so, and when he began building the first railway lines in the Midlands he became very wealthy,' said Terence and, with a grin, he added: 'However, the poor old major came to a sad end in the Headingley railway disaster of 1864.'

I looked at him with a frown. 'Terence Whiter, you should be ashamed of yourself,' I said severely. 'How can the demise of your relative be a subject of levity?'

He threw up his hands in surrender at my rebuke. 'Sorry, Miss Rosie, I suppose I shouldn't laugh about it but when I found out the way he departed this mortal coil I simply

titties, sucking at her engorged nipples as she pressed him to her. His trousers were down to his knees and the sun flashed across his white bottom as he raised himself up before plunging his prick inside her cunney. She raised her well-made thighs and her strong legs clasped themselves around his waist in a vice-like grip. The rise and fall of his arse now increased to a frenzied pace and I saw the girl's hips lifting clear off the grass as she forced his cock even deeper inside her honeypot.

'Have a closer look,' I said as I passed the glasses over to my young fellow traveller, and I could hardly help noticing the huge bulge which had formed in Terence's trousers.

The engine whistle blew and we began to move slowly forward. Terence kept the binoculars trained on the fornicating pair until they were out of vision and then he dropped them from his eyes and said hoarsely: 'By God, I wish that it were me under that tree! But with my luck I'll be as old as the major on his last fuck with Nellie Clifton.'

'Now what makes you say that, Terence? You are a good-looking young chap and I am certain that when the time is right there will be no shortage of girls ready to initiate you into the joys of *l'art de faire l'amour*.'

'I very much doubt it,' he replied gloomily. 'It's true that Patricia, the maid who was involved in my expulsion from Eton, is now in service at my Aunt Gwen's, but if I know anything about my Uncle Eric, he'll be fucking her at every opportunity and I won't find it easy to win back her favours.'

'That would be most unfortunate,' I said, laying my hand on Terence's knee. 'Lord Philip Pelham told me of the circumstances which led to your plight and I must say that in my opinion you did nothing to warrant such a severe punishment.'

'Thank you, but I do seem to have had my share of bad

luck. I did think that I was going to cross the Rubicon only a few nights after I was sent down from Eton, but although I almost achieved my goal, at the very last Dame Fortune refused to smile upon me.'

'You poor boy! Why, what happened?' I enquired with genuine solicitude in my voice, for I did feel sorry for him, although I readily confess that I was equally keen to hear what promised to be an interesting erotic anecdote! 'Don't be bashful, Terence, you can share any intimate secret with me,' I said, letting my fingertips run lightly down his leg.

His face coloured slightly at this but he did continue, saying: 'It was on a Saturday evening and my parents had invited several members of the family to dine with us. I was sitting next to my cousin Molly, a pretty, fair-haired girl who had only the previous week celebrated her eighteenth birthday. She was wearing a low-cut gown and during dinner I could hardly keep my eyes from the swell of her luscious breasts which sat so temptingly inside her soft silk dress.

'After dinner I asked Molly if she would care to play table-tennis with me and, with our parents' approval, we left the lounge and scuttled upstairs to the games room. Once we were alone she looked mischievously at me and said with a little giggle: "Oh, Terry, you really are a naughty boy."

' "Me? Naughty? Why do you say that?" I asked and she answered boldly: "Well, for a start, during the meal you made it very obvious how interested you were in my bosoms."

'I was taken aback by her forthright reply and blushed deeply as I mumbled a few words of apology.

' "No, you really don't have to apologise, you silly thing," Molly breathed as she pulled me closer to her. "At least, so long as you can prove to me that it was my looks which were making such a bulge in your lap and not anyone else's."

'I could hardly believe my ears, but when she pressed

herself against me and kissed me full on the lips I decided that further words were not needed and I returned her kiss, taking the lovely creature into my arms.

'Our lips opened and we wiggled our tongues inside each other's mouths, and then Molly stepped back a pace and unhooked the catch at the back of her dress. She stepped out of the garment which fell to the floor and my shaft pressed against my trousers so forcefully that it threatened to tear through the material. Then she pulled her white chemise over her head and my heart began to pound as she bared her beautiful, rounded breasts with their erect, quivering nipples, and I had to steady myself by leaning against the wall when she stepped out of her shoes and stood naked before me except for her stocking belt and frilly lace panties.

'With a sensual smile she tugged down the front of her drawers just an inch or two to let me catch a glimpse of her golden pussey bush and she whispered: "Would you like to see more, Terry?"

'All I could do was to nod my head, for I was now far too excited to give a coherent reply. Molly gave me another wicked grin and went on: "Very well, you may in a minute then, but let's first make ourselves comfortable."

'We sat ourselves down on the sofa and resumed our embrace and now Molly let her fingers fall directly on my throbbing tool and rubbed it with the palm of her hand. I tore off my jacket and unbuckled the belt of my trousers whilst she nimbly unfastened the buttons of my flies. I lifted my hips and she pulled them down together with my drawers so that my naked prick and balls were exposed to her view.

' "Oh, my God!" I gasped as she grasped hold of my swollen shaft and moved her body across and downwards to kneel in front of me. Then she leaned forward and licked all around my knob before opening her mouth and sucking in my tool between her soft, wet lips. She sucked and sucked, slowly and skilfully, teasing my balls with her fingernails, twirling her tongue round my knob, biting, lapping, kissing. This was so stimulating that she only had time to bob her head a couple of times up and down my rigid rod before I was ready to shoot my seed down her throat.

'Molly understood my urgent need to spunk and she gave my balls a gentle queeze and this made me explode immediately, sending a rush of seed through my twitching tadger gushing into her willing mouth. My cock pulsed wildly as she happily swallowed my sticky emission, milking my trembling tool of every last drop of jism, and then she licked her lips and said: "Gracious, you *are* a big boy, Terry. Why, your dickie is still almost as hard as before I sucked it. Let me see if I can make it rise up again to its full height."

'I stood there dazed as she added: "Oh dear, my pussey is so wet that I must take off my knickers or my skin will become chapped." And with that she slowly pulled down her panties, and at the sight of her damp thatch of blonde pussey hair, my prick swelled back up to a bursting erection and Molly scrambled to her feet and threw herself back on the sofa with her legs wide apart.'

Terence wiped his brow and I exclaimed: 'For heaven's sake, Terence Whiter, what further invitation could you have wanted? So what did you do then? Ask her if she wanted to play ping-pong?'

'No I did not!' he snapped at me. 'But just as I was about to climb on top of her I heard footsteps on the stairs and I sprang across the room to switch off the electric light and we hid behind the sofa. The door opened and my father came in and called: "Hello there, anyone in?"

'We waited with bated breath until he closed the door and then dressed ourselves in record speed. We managed to creep downstairs and when asked where we had been, we made some excuse about teasing my father by playing hide-and-seek with him.

'So there you are, Miss Rosie,' he concluded unhappily. 'My best chance of becoming a man was stymied by a cruel twist of fate. I feel so despondent thinking about it that I wonder if I am doomed to remain celibate for the rest of my life!'

'Stuff and nonsense!' I replied robustly. 'Mark my words, I'll wager you a pound to a penny that you'll lose your unwanted virginity in the Eternal City. Sit at a pavement café and watch the world go by in the *passegiata*, the ritual evening parade, and I guarantee that you will soon need an extra pillow for a bed-mate.'

Terence lapsed into a sulky silence for he thought that I was merely humouring him, though it is a fact that many young people of both sexes whom I count as close friends have enjoyed intimate, forbidden escapades in this lovely country. However, he cheered up as we approached the environs of the city and Signor Nettolone was on the station platform to welcome us, holding up a placard with our names above his head so that we would be able to recognise him.

Carlo Nettolone was a handsome, swarthy gentleman of about thirty years of age with curly black hair, deep dark eyes and when he smiled a greeting to me he showed a perfect set of gleaming white teeth that were set off so strikingly against his olive complexion.

'*Buon giorno, Signorina d'Argosse, Signor Whiter, benvenuto a Roma*,' he beamed, shaking our hands. 'I have Dino, my servant here to attend to your luggage. Leave everything to him and follow me.'

Obediently we followed him and we travelled in a convoy of three motor cars directly to his villa where he lived with Fiona Robson, a charming American lady and a noted photographer from New York who had been commissioned by a publisher to produce work for a new illustrated guidebook to Italy. Carlo Nettolone was a bachelor but to my relief he made no attempt to conceal his relationship with Fiona, perhaps knowing that anyone with any connections to either King Edward VII or Count Gewirtz of Galicia would have to be of a broadminded and tolerant disposition.

After Terence and I were shown to our bedrooms and given the chance to refresh ourselves, I hastened to pass a heavy brown envelope to Carlo from the Count, thus fulfilling our part of the arrangement with Johnny Gewirtz who, as he had promised, had not only given young Terence fifty pounds spending money but had in addition wired me the same amount to the Savoy in London before we set off. And he had also paid all our travelling expenses, and Carlo was quick to inform me when I asked to be allowed to contribute to the expenses of the household that he had taken it upon himself to reimburse Carlo for entertaining Terence and myself.

We dined simply on *Zuppa Pavese* (a clear soup with eggs poached in it), *Gnocchi* (poached dumplings made from flour, cheese and eggs), followed by *Trotelle all'Italiana* (trout baked with fennel and wine). We drank the famous Est! Est! Est! white wine from Montefioscone and we finished our repast with ice cream and fresh fruit.

'Thank you for a delicious meal,' I said to Fiona as Carlo and Terence rose from the table to take a post-prandial stroll in the gardens.

'Ah, for that you have to thank Angelica. She is a superb cook and I don't know what we would do without her, although employing her does have a strange drawback.'

However, just as I was about to ask what that might be, an ear-piercing yell made me nearly jump out of my skin. It had floated up from the kitchen and I was concerned that mayhem was being committed down there, but Fiona put her hand on my arm and said with a smile: 'Don't be alarmed, Rosie, there is nothing to worry about. You must

156

forgive me, for I should have warned you before we sat down at the table that we might hear such noises after dinner.'

Another tremendous shriek rent the air and I gasped: 'But for heaven's sake, who is responsible for that din?' and Fiona chuckled as she replied in a surprisingly casual fashion: 'I'm afraid that it's Angelica enjoying her regular Wednesday evening fuck with Father Lionel.'

This shocked me to the core. 'With a priest?' I echoed in amazement, but Fiona explained herself further: 'Ah, I realise that this may sound somewhat scandalous to you, but then Father Lionel is a rather unusual man of the cloth. He is the chief pastor in Rome of the Worldwide Epicurean Church to which Angelica belongs.'

She saw the blank look on my face and kindly continued: 'The Epicureans follow the teachings of their mentor, the Greek philosopher Epicurus who held that the pursuit of pleasure is the highest good. In the case of our cook, this is being fucked doggie-style by Father Lionel who spends much of his time making himself available for such pastoral duties.'

'Quite a screamer, isn't she?' I remarked whilst I digested Fiona's information about this unusual organisation, and then I added hastily. 'Not that I mind the noise, for the sounds of a lusty couple enjoying themselves can be quite exciting. I don't suppose we could have a look, could we?'

'Certainly we could,' said Fiona, rising to her feet as another yell assaulted our ears. 'Come downstairs with me. Angelica won't mind at all, although at this stage I would imagine she will be far too busy with Father Lionel's prick to notice us.'

We descended the stairs into the kitchen where Angelica, a well-made girl of not more than twenty-five, was standing nude in front of the kitchen table, bending forward with her arms outstretched and her fingers curled round the edges of the table. The quivering white globes of her bottom stuck out saucily whilst behind her was a slight gentleman who was pistoning his glistening boner in and out of the cleft between the cheeks of her luscious arse and, with every vigorous thrust, he buried his cock to the hilt, his heavy balls banging against her heaving, rounded buttocks.

The girl's plump backside slapped nicely against his thighs as she fitted easily into the rhythm of Father Lionel's fucking. Again she shrieked with pleasure as his gleaming shaft see-sawed in and out of her dripping crack. Reaching behind her, Angelica caressed his wrinkled pink ballsack as she rocked to and fro, her head thrown back and her hair whipping from side to side as she called out: '*Dio mio, mio caro Lionel, più, più, per favore*!'

She wriggled her bottom in a wild frenzy, her hips rotating to achieve the maximum penetration and then she threw back her head in total abandon as she let out a final, uninhibited whoop of passion as she climaxed. Seconds later, Father Lionel's wiry torso stiffened and with an anguished cry he made one final, gigantic thrust forwards, his balls slapping against the back of Angelica's thighs before he pulled out his prick and spurted spasm after spasm of hot, frothy spunk over her bum cheeks.

'Note how the good padre ensures that he does not spend inside her cunney, as the silly girl hasn't taken any precautions,' commented Fiona as Angelica handed her ecclesiastical paramour a dishcloth to wipe his seed from her buttocks, and Father Lionel turned to us and said in a broad American twang: 'Yeah, I'm always telling girls to follow that maxim of the Boy Scouts, *be prepared*, Fiona, if they don't want to be put in the family way.'

So this athletic young man of the cloth hailed from the United States and I wondered how he came to be in Rome. In the meantime, Fiona introduced him to me and, after accepting our invitation to join us upstairs, he gave Angelica a farewell kiss and a friendly pat on the rump as the sultry girl dressed herself.

Back on the verandah, Fiona poured out cognac for Lionel whilst she and I sipped *strega* and I made so bold as to ask my question aloud and asked where he had been ordained.

'Well now, I guess ordination isn't quite the right word,' he drawled as we sat ourselves down in the comfortable easy chairs. 'To be absolutely honest, the Worldwide Epicurean Church is hardly a religious organisation in the strict sense of the word. It's more of a fraternity, but by making the club a church, our subscriptions, or donations, as we prefer to call them, can be set against income tax.'

'So people of all faiths may join the Epicureans without compromising their religion?' I said and Father Lionel nodded. 'Certainly they may, Miss d'Argosse. I happen to be a Methodist, but back in the States we have in our ranks Protestants of all denominations, Catholics and Jews. We refuse to operate any restriction on the grounds of race, colour or creed and in the East, for example, we can boast of many Muslims, Sikhs and Hindus within our ranks. The Maharajah of Lockshenstan is an honoured member, as is Prince Mumsahbedanida of Mesopotamia.

'In England, we also have a number of *sub rosa* adherents including the entire committee of the Jim Jam Club [*a notorious high class salle privée in Great Windmill Street patronised by, amongst others, Edward VII and Mr Lloyd-George – Editor*] and we have just opened a chapter of the organisation here in Rome. In fact, the reason you find me here is because as one of the few full-time officials of the order, I am supervising the opening party which will be held next week.'

'I suppose that the Epicureans is only for men,' I remarked, but Father Lionel shook his head and said: 'Certainly not, my dear, we welcome women, and if you

159

are interested I will enrol you here and now as a member of our British branch. Fiona joined us last month and I think I may safely say she has already received good value for her annual subscription of one hundred dollars. It's a great deal of money, I know, but those less well-off like Angelica are charged only a nominal sum.'

At this point I saw Carlo and Terence sauntering back through the garden and I said hastily: 'That young lad walking beside Signor Nettolone would benefit from membership for he is quite desperate to lose his virginity, but circumstances have militated against his achieving this ambition.'

'Well now, Miss d'Argosse, you must understand that the Epicurean Church is much more than a glorified house of pleasure,' said Father Lionel stiffly. 'We organise concerts, conversaziones, and many cultural activities and we donate thousands of dollars to charitable institutions around the globe. On the other hand, we do pride ourselves on lending a hand whenever possible — but to the needy, not the greedy.'

'Oh, Terence falls very much in the former category,' I said with a twinkle in my eye. 'It would do him the world of good to relieve his frustrations with a young lady who could instruct him in the sensual arts.'

Father Lionel stroked his chin and then said quietly to me: 'After I leave this evening, tell the boy to come to forty-seven, Via Trippetto, at noon tomorrow and tell the maid he has an appointment with Signorina Sophia.'

Carlo and Terence now joined us and I should have mentioned before that my fascinating new acquaintance was wearing a cassock and, whilst we sat chatting of this and that, Terence respectfully addressed him as Father until the Epicurean said: 'There's no need to call me Father, my boy, as actually I'm not even a Christian clergyman let alone a Catholic priest.'

Naturally Terence was very surprised and so Lionel continued: 'I rather enjoy dressing in clerical garb as, generally speaking, I've found that I've been treated far more politely by everyone from shopkeepers to the police.'

'That may well be, but I'm not certain that your practice is legal,' mused Carlo, who as I later discovered was one of the most distinguished lawyers in Rome, which is how he came to be recommended to Count Gewirtz.

'Probably not, said Lionel cheerfully, 'but then so many of life's pleasures are similarly frowned upon by society. However, I suspect I do far less harm than many in Holy Orders, my philosophy being that of enjoying oneself to the full – though at the same time always taking the utmost care to ensure that no-one is ever harmed by one's behaviour.'

He rose up to leave but Fiona placed her hand on his arm and said: 'Oh, don't go, Lionel, it's only half past ten. Perhaps you would stay for a few hands of bridge.'

'It is a little late for a game, isn't it?' he said, but after I noticed Fiona wink at him, he changed his mind and sat down again.

'If you are going to play bridge, may I be excused?' said Terence politely. 'It's been a long day and I can hardly keep my eyes open.'

We wished him good night and I walked into the lounge with Terence and whispered Father Lionel's message to him. He looked puzzled, so I told him that I would explain everything to him at breakfast the following morning. When I returned to the others on the verandah I expected Fiona to be searching for some playing cards, but instead the others were standing up as if ready to come back inside the villa.

In all innocence I asked: 'Aren't we playing outside? It's a very warm evening and we could set up a card table on the verandah.'

Fiona laughed and took me to one side. 'Rosie, I didn't

161

have cards in mind when I asked Lionel to stay. The truth of the matter is that I'm really in the mood for a little dancing. I'll put on the gramophone as I'm dying to hear the new ragtime records my sister has sent me from New York. Would you like to partner Carlo whilst I take the floor with Lionel?'

'It will be my pleasure,' I said and it really was delightful dancing with Carlo who whirled me elegantly round the room to the lively music. Then we took a breather and sat on the sofa watching Fiona and Lionel holding each other very tightly and swaying to a tune in a far slower tempo. I felt somewhat ill at ease looking at them but when I glanced across at Carlo, he put a finger to his mouth and slipped his arms round my waist as he said: 'Don't be concerned, Lionel is one of our best friends and Fiona has my permission to enjoy herself as she pleases.'

This was just as well, for Lionel had guided Fiona onto the sofa opposite us and his hands were busily running over her breasts whilst her own hands had raised his cassock and were hauling down his drawers. He gave a gasp which I assumed signalled that Fiona had grabbed hold of his thick prick and he then pulled the cassock over his head to reveal that this was indeed the case.

He helped Fiona tear off her clothes until she, too, was naked and then she rolled Lionel over onto his back. Her mop of beautiful chestnut hair disappeared between his legs, lightly touching his balls as she kissed and sucked his enormous erection. He groaned with delight as she stayed on her knees, licking and lapping the uncapped ruby helmet of his pulsating prick, and as she leaned over to take more of the blue-veined shaft between her lips, her luscious backside moved sensuously from side to side.

'Rosie, how would you like to join them?' whispered Carlo. 'Fiona adores being licked out, and I would love to see you eat her pussey.'

The sight of the young couple had fired my senses and I needed no second bidding. Carlo helped me strip off my clothes and I carefully positioned myself behind Fiona. She wriggled with pleasure as I squeezed her deliciously soft bum cheeks and then I turned myself round to lie on my back in the same direction as Lionel and slid my head underneath her and, without further ado, I began to lick the silky thatch of pussey hair which lightly covered the pouting lips of her cunney.

Fiona sucked lustily on Lionel's cock whilst I now slipped my tongue inside her cunt and, avoiding her clitty, I lapped steadily away on her vaginal walls and tasted the mushy wetness of her love juice. I heard Lionel moan: 'Christ, I'm coming, I'm coming, I can't stop now!' and as she swallowed his jets of salty jism I nipped her clitty gently with my teeth and, as spasms of pure ecstasy shot through her body, I continued to fuck her sopping pussey with my tongue, lapping up her cuntal juices which were now pouring out of her dripping crack.

Meanwhile Carlo had now undressed and had padded over to join us. Stripped, Carlo looked even more attractive — his torso was quite hairy and his cock looked very exciting, not perhaps the biggest I have ever seen but certainly of a fine length, sticking upwards at an angle with the foreskin slipped back to reveal a well-formed, purple helmet. I had no time to notice any more for immediately he positioned himself carefully between my open legs. He began by kneading my breasts and almost before I could catch my breath, his head was between my legs, nestling in my blonde bush. His tongue was soon at work on my moist honeypot, flicking and licking, lapping and slurping against my pouting pussey lips which swiftly opened to allow him to suck on my clitty.

My excitement grew stronger as I lovingly clutched his head, murmuring my approval as his lips pressed against my cunt. He slid his tongue up and around, sucking my clitty as I ground my slit against his mouth, feeling my love button emerge from its protective sheath and rise up in size like a miniature penis. He flicked it so expertly with his tongue that I came very quickly, my juices dousing his face as he eagerly lapped up the sweet flow.

'I'm ready for your prick now, Carlo,' I whimpered and seconds later I thrilled to the feel of his fat knob parting my pussey lips. I lifted my thighs and Carlo's cock slid straight into my love channel, deeper and deeper until his balls slapped against my bum and I worked my legs upwards, wrapping them around his back as, slowly and with great deliberation, he fucked me with his gorgeous, stiff truncheon.

'*Bello! Bello! Bello!*' Carlo cried as he upped the tempo, pumping furiously into my juicy cunt as his heavy balls banged away on my bum until his tool trembled inside my cunt and we melted away in a sea of sperm, his sticky seed mingling with my own love liquids which flowed freely from my tingling cunney.

We lay still in what would have been a superb *pose plastique* with Lionel flat on his back, his flaccid prick still jammed inside Fiona's mouth as the pretty girl knelt between his legs, her own thighs open to accommodate me, whilst Carlo lay on top of me, his throbbing tool still semi-erect even after spewing out such a copious spunky emission.

As is not unusual in these situations, the so-called superior males were *hors de combat* and needed time to recover, although Fiona and I were more than ready for a further helping of cock and Fiona looked reproachfully at our gallants as she slid her fingers around their limp shafts and squeezed them. But both pricks stayed soft and with a disdainful look at the two crestfallen cocks, she sighed: 'Rosie, I'm afraid that we shall just have to amuse ourselves until these two gentlemen recover,' and I replied lustfully: 'No matter, I'm happy to lie back and enjoy whatever might come my way.'

'We'd all be a lot more comfortable in bed,' observed Lionel as he slid himself out from under Fiona and rolled onto the carpet, and we took up this sensible suggestion and crept upstairs into Carlo and Fiona's bedroom.

'Lie down, Rosie,' instructed my hostess and so I placed a pillow under my head and reclined on the soft mattress, lewdly raising and parting my thighs so that my pussey was open and inviting to all who wished to see it. Fiona jumped on the bed and sat on her knees in front of me as she eased her hands under the firm, resilient cheeks of my bottom as I raised my hips towards her pretty face.

Without hesitation she buried her mouth in my silky thatch of golden hair before sliding the tip of her tongue between my cunney lips. Licking and sucking with a delicate touch, she brought me to the very edge of a spend in no time at all. But then she withdrew her tongue and ran her long forefinger down the length of my puffy crack.

'Look at the parting of Rosie's love lips,' she said to Carlo and Lionel. 'They proclaim her need for a thick, stiff prick to slide in between them. Surely one of you is ready to give this young girl what she wants?'

I was pleased that Lionel's prick was the first to stand stiffly to attention, for whilst Carlo's cock did a fine job, variety is the spice of life and I doubted if I would be given another chance to sample the member of the Epicurean minister which had already performed sterling service, not only with Fiona, but also in the servants' quarters with the cook.

Anyway, Lionel gave his thick prick a shake and then clambered on top of me. He placed his knob against my blonde muff and rubbed it up and down against my cunney lips, which I found extremely stimulating. I reached down and guided his shaft inside my honeypot and, once he was fully embedded, I wrapped my legs around his waist and urged him onwards.

We struck up a good rhythm from the beginning and as his lusty cock slewed in and out of my juicy pussey, his fingers worked in unison over my engorged raspberry nipples. Oh how superbly Father Lionel fucked me, his whole body moving with such easy grace, sending thrills of delight inside my tingling cunt again and again as he pistoned his marvellous prick inside the innermost depths of my cunt.

He moved his hands to my bottom, holding my bum cheeks and massaging them with each stroke of his marvellous cock, and steadily the pace of this wonderful joust increased as we thrust against each other, our hearts and minds joined together in the intensity of these magnificent moments.

Suddenly I felt the first, long-drawn-out shudder of my approaching spend sweep over me. And now Lionel's prick began to tremble and, when I realised that he too was approaching his climax, I reached down and cradled his balls. This caused his body to go rigid and he exploded into me in a rush of liquid fire. It was my turn to shiver all over as I felt the first surge of frothy seed flood into my cunt and then my entire body was bathed in a glorious, warm sensation as Lionel's creamy injection filled my love channel. Gripping him with my thighs, I forced his throbbing tool even deeper inside my cunt and with every throb of his majestic penis, wonderful waves of utter bliss rippled through my body.

'More! More! More!' I cried out, desperate to prolong this blissful feeling and, gamely, Lionel drove on as I milked his prick of the last spurts of his copious emission. One last joint spasm racked our bodies until he collapsed on top of me and I could feel his proud shaft now deflating inside my drenched cunney.

I rolled him off me and he lay on his back, his chest still heaving from the physical efforts of our love-making (Dr Letchmore once informed me that in terms of exercising the body, a good fuck is the equivalent of a brisk, two-mile run). I hauled myself up and bent over to lick the remaining drops of jism from the tip of his now-shrivelled cock as his knob disappeared under the cover of his foreskin, like a rabbit fleeing into its warren. I ran my hands over his hairy balls and rubbed them in the stickiness of his crinkly pubic hair. At first he was puzzled by my action, but then he understood my intentions when I held his wrists lightly and pressed his hands to my own pubic thatch. Taking this cue from me, Lionel rubbed and fondled my pussey until I raised his fingers to my lips and I licked my own love fluids from him.

Fiona was now eager for further frolics, but alas poor Carlo was still unable to maintain a rock-hard stiffie. So shucking off her robe, she threw herself down beside me and, twisting me upon my hip, the pretty girl whispered for me to relax whilst her soft, nude body cuddled closer to mine.

I lay shimmering with pleasure whilst she sucked my tongue into her mouth and we clung together, our hands roaming over each other's breasts, our nipples flaring up into hard little bullets against our hands. We revelled in our kissing and hugging and then Fiona moved her lips downwards to lick my titties, and then even lower to glide her tongue inside my sopping cleft, prodding my clitty as she brought me off in a little series of electric shivers which ran up and down my spine.

Then she raised herself on top of me, pressing her nubile young body hard against me and our hands were now everywhere, pinching, grabbing, squeezing as our bodies melted together, demanding an early release. The adorable girl jerked her thick, curly-fleeced cunt savagely against my own moist muff and our pussies rubbed lubriciously together

167

until Fiona looked up and saw that her partner had climbed onto his knees beside us and from the state of his shaft, which was standing smartly to attention almost vertically up against his flat belly, Carlo was at last ready for the fray.

However, having waited so long for the arrival of Carlo's cock, Fiona was determined to extract the maximum pleasure from his love truncheon. She hauled herself off me and swung round to present herself on all fours, with her lovely bottom just inches away from my face. She turned her pretty head round and said to me: 'Rosie, as you probably agree, it's even nicer when the prick follows the tongue. Would you prepare my cunt for Carlo's cock by licking me out before he fucks me?'

'With the greatest of pleasure, dear Fiona,' I replied and I parted the soft cheeks of her glorious backside and slid my tongue inside the cleft between them. The tip of my tongue tickled the lips of her dripping crack whilst I stabbed my forefinger in and out of her cunney with a fierce intensity which caused her to cry out with delight.

I moved my tongue along the rolled grooves of her pussey and she moved slightly backwards to sit upon my face whilst I sucked her tangy cuntal juices which were now cascading out of her cunney.

It would not have been too difficult to finish her off, but Carlo was waiting impatiently to stake his claim so I lifted Fiona's bum from my lips and rolled over to the side to let him continue this lascivious spooning.

They lay on their sides facing each other and I sat up to see Carlo's hand cup one of her jutting bosoms and Fiona take her partner's glistening stiffstander between her fingers, her hand working up and down the swollen shaft. Her nipples seemed to grow before my very eyes as Carlo fondled each of her proud, naked breasts. Now he moved his head from side to side, kissing each luscious tittie whilst his right arm reached down to let his fingers toy in the silky chestnut mass of hair at the base of her belly or slide directly into the crimson chink buried in its folds.

Fiona rolled her head from side to side on the pillow and groaned with joy as he continued to suck on her raised-up raspberry nipples, whilst ever so lightly his fingers traced the open wet slit of her cunney, flicking the tiny, erect clitty which was now peeping out.

'Fuck me, Carlo! Ram your Roman rod inside my juicy pussey,' she cried out, and being ever-ready to give a helping hand, I leaned forward, grasped Carlo's cock in my hand and inserted the wide, purple helmet between her pink, pouting pussey lips. He pressed forward slowly, propelling in inch after inch until their pubic hairs were matted together, and then he pulled back before quickly driving forward the full length of his pulsating prick inside her delectable honeypot again and again.

She urged him on, closing her feet together at the small of his back to force even more of his throbbing tool inside her clinging cunney, and Lionel moved over to sit next to me to watch Carlo's quivering cock work in and out of Fiona's sopping sheath, her love lips opening and closing over the fleshy lollipop which was pleasuring her cunney so exquisitely.

Carlo was now panting with exertion as he rammed home his gleaming shaft, which pistoned at speed in and out of Fiona's drenched crack, his muscular body rocking backwards and forwards between her thighs. Fiona shuddered into a glorious spend whilst Carlo fucked her at an ever-increasing rate of knots. She raked her fingernails down his back as she thrilled to the voluptuous sensations of his big cock pumping in and out of her cunt until, with a hoarse roar, he spurted a fierce flow of hot, sticky seed into her welcoming womb.

Father Lionel stayed the night with me in the Nettolone bedroom with Fiona and Carlo and we spent the small hours

169

in various whoresome foursomes, my favourite perhaps being that of being bum-fucked by Carlo whilst on my knees sucking Lionel's balls as he lay flat on his back with Fiona bouncing up and down on his rigid, upright cock. Also to my taste was the arrangement of our bodies when we woke up the next morning. This finished up with me lying on top of and slightly across Fiona, our hairy pussies grinding together as I sucked her horny titties whilst using both my hands to toss off Carlo's cock, slicking my hands up and down his veiny shaft, and Fiona gobbled on Lionel's knob which he had inserted between her rich, red lips as he knelt by her side.

Surprisingly, I was not tired after I left my fellow revellers and, after taking a refreshing warm shower, I dressed myself and on the landing I saw a servant girl, carrying a tray of croissants and coffee, about to knock on young Terence Whiter's door. This reminded me to speak to the young scamp about his appointment at noon with Signorina Sophia.

'Here, I'll carry that into his bedroom,' I said to the maid, lifting the tray out of her hands. '*Bene, Signorina*,' she replied with a curtsy and I knocked on the door and strode straight in.

Of course it was inexcusable not to wait for Terence to shout 'come in' and he had every right to be angry about my unwarranted interruption. For as he did not immediately realise I had come in, he continued to play with his prick unaware that I was watching him finish himself off in the final stage of his early-morning masturbation. He was lying naked on the bed, pumping his fist up and down his erect shaft and, with a little grunt, he climaxed in front of me, and I looked on with interest as the gummy essence spurted out from his knob onto his belly and curly pubic hair which surrounded the base of his prick.

'Oh, damn and blast!' he cried out when he suddenly

realised that I was standing in front of the bed, and he covered himself with the eiderdown.

'Good morning, Terence, did you sleep well?' I said in as neutral a voice as I could muster. 'I just thought I would remind you of your appointment at noon with Signorina Sophia. Would you like to take a walk through the city with me this morning? It so happens that it would be most convenient for me to go with you to Via Trippetto, as Fiona has recommended a fashion house in the Piazza de Souza which is only round the corner from where you are bound.'

'Yes, thank you, Miss Rosie, thank you very much,' he stammered out as I turned on my heel and went out, taking care to close the door behind me.

An hour or so later, the Nettolone's chauffeur drove us through to the centre of the city and Terence and I wandered happily through the bustling streets towards the Piazza di Spagna. In my humble opinion, there is no other city in Europe which can rival the unique attractions of Rome — such an intensely alive city where people live, work and enjoy themselves in and among colour-washed medieval tenements, Renaissance palazzi and the marble columns of ancient times.

We made our way up the Spanish Steps through the Borghese Gardens to the Villa Borghese, built in the early seventeenth century by Cardinal Scipione Borghese, which houses his fine collection of paintings and sculpture as well as the best pieces sold by Camillo Borghese to his brother-in-law, Napoleon, in 1807.

There was not time to visit the Villa this morning but I said to Terence: 'One day you must spend a day there. There is one particular statue by Canova which I know you would find especially interesting. I am referring to a most provocative nude study of Napoleon's beautiful sister, Pauline, who was married to Prince Borghese, but she was

171

reputed to have had a string of lovers and was the cause of much scandalous gossip.'

He grinned as he pulled out his pocket watch and said: 'I'll certainly bear that in mind, Miss Rosie — but I think we had better walk back to Via Trippetto as I don't want to be late for my appointment with this mysterious Signorina Sophia.'

So we returned to the Spanish Steps and at the bottom turned into the Via della Croce and a hundred yards further along we found ourselves at the junction with Via Trippetto.

'I'll leave you here,' I said brightly. 'And let's rendezvous over there at Otello's restaurant between half past one and two o'clock.'

This would give him enough time to enter the gates of Elysium, I thought to myself as I waved goodbye and strolled round the corner into the elegant Piazza de Souza and soon found *Di Sylvana*, the exclusive shop which Fiona had insisted I visit adding, rather oddly I thought, that I would be certain to enjoy the experience.

The small shopfront was richly dressed with what appeared to be the latest in fashionable apparel, and as I entered the shop I was welcomed by an extremely attractive girl of about my own age with a finely formed face on which was perched a mass of shiny brown hair which fell down in ringlets upon her shoulders. Her eyes were also a deep shade of brown and her tight blouse accentuated a pair of high, thrusting bosoms which I noticed with a tad of envy were probably slightly larger than my own.

She was wearing a beige linen skirt which further accentuated her tanned complexion and she greeted me with a pleasant smile. '*Buon giorno, Signorina,*' she said and I returned her smile: ' '*Parliamo inglese, per favore?*' I asked and she nodded and said in perfect, if slightly accented, English: 'Yes, I can speak English, though not as well as I would like. But I am happy to say that many British and

American ladies come to this shop and I have many opportunities to practise the language. May I ask, did one of these ladies recommend that you visited me?'

'Yes, Signorina Fiona Robson told me that I was certain to find something I would like in your shop,' I answered as I looked around the crowded room which was stocked with racks of gowns as well as many bolts of material. 'I presume that this is your shop, signorina?'

'It is indeed. I am Sylvana Vitelli, the prioprietor of this establishment,' she said with a sweep of her hand. 'And whom do I have the honour of serving this afternoon?'

I introduced myself and Sylvana put her hand to her mouth as her brow furrowed. 'D'Argosse . . . d'Argosse . . . this name is very familiar to me. Ah, I think I have it. May I ask, have you ever made the acquaintance of Countess Marussia of Samarkand?'

Had I ever made the acquaintance of Countess Marussia of Samarkand?! Readers of my previous set of recollections [*Rosie 2: 'Young, Wild And Willing − Editor*] will surely need no reminder of the uninhibited orgy Lord Philip Pelham and I attended at the Countess's house in Mayfair, and I wondered just how well Signorina Sylvana knew the sensuous Countess and her escort, the charming Prince Adrian of the Netherlands.

My unasked question was soon answered by this dark, voluptuous girl who smiled at me and, as she looked directly into my eyes, said: 'On my last visit to London, the Marquis de Soveral [*the suave Portuguese chargé d'affaires in London and a great favourite in London Society − Editor*] escorted me to a secret party at the Countess's house in Grosvenor Square. Perhaps you have been to such a gathering, Miss d'Argosse?'

'Yes, I have had that pleasure,' I said carefully and she added boldly: 'May I take it, then, that like myself you were also fucked by either Prince Adrian or the Countess?'

'To be honest, I cannot exactly remember who was had by whom,' I confessed with a giggle. 'But obviously we both attended the same sort of party, even if the guests were different.'

'In that case, I know just the sort of clothes that will interest you, Signorina Rosie,' said Sylvana as she skipped to the door of the shop and turned the key in the lock. Then she pulled down the window blind, which still let plenty of light through into the shop, and went on: 'There, that will give us some privacy. Now would you excuse me a moment, I must change my dress.'

I looked blankly at her and she explained: 'I model our creations myself for my favourite clients so they can see what my clothes look like from all angles before deciding whether or not to place an order for my staff to make up the garments especially for them.'

With that she disappeared behind a red curtain into the rear of the shop. 'Please stay where you are, Signorina Rosie,' she called out brightly. 'I will ask you to join me in just a few moments.'

There was a rustling sound behind the curtain and after only a minute or so, Sylvana's hand came round the side of the curtain and beckoned me into the inner sanctum. I pulled the curtain to one side and caught my breath. She was wearing a silk *robe de nuit*, a wide sweeping garment with ruffles which was held together only by a sash around her waist. She stepped towards me and from her luscious body I could smell the exquisite aroma of an expensive perfume which she must have dabbed upon her swelling, white breasts.

'This is a nightgown I made for Fiona Robson — although she says she usually goes to bed in the nude, for Carlo is a very passionate gentleman!

'But this is such a charming robe, so sensual is it not?' she said swivelling round coquettishly.

174

'Both the robe and the model are stunning,' I replied softly and at once Sylvana tugged at the sash and untied the simple knot. The gown opened, it fell to the ground, and Sylvana stepped forward towards me in all her naked glory. I caught my breath as she stood before me, like a statue crafted by a master sculptor come magically to life. Below the mass of sultry dark hair and her pouting pretty face, beautiful full breasts stood out proudly, whilst between her perfectly proportioned thighs lay a lustrous veil of dark, silky hair which contrasted so delightfully with the snowy whiteness of her belly.

Sylvana turned on her heel and went over to bend over a small ice-box which gave me the opportunity to admire the pert, spherical *rondeurs* of her delicious bum cheeks. From the ice-box she took out a tray upon which stood a bottle of Asti Spumante and two tall glasses.

'Good heavens, do you always stop work for a drink in the middle of the day? What a splendid custom!' I said as Sylvana opened the bottle and the cork flew out with a 'pop'.

'Only on special occasions, like when entertaining new friends,' she murmured as she passed me a glass of the sparkling, fizzy wine which we clinked together before sipping at our refreshingly cold drinks. 'Now, would you like to undress and try on this robe?'

Well, to cut short this story, we finished the bottle before I undressed, but as I stood in front of the mirror I twisted round to view my bottom.

'Oh dear, I'm afraid that my backside is getting just the tiniest bit flabby,' I declared but Sylvana stepped behind me and ran her hands over my dimpled cheeks as she breathed: 'No, no, not at all, Rosie, you have a superb *derrière*. You have a gorgeous bottom which is begging to be squeezed. Oh, how smooth and so firm it is!

'There, isn't that nice?' she asked as she gently caressed my buttocks in her hands.

175

'Very nice indeed,' I said softly as I turned round and we stood silently for a moment facing each other, so close that our nipples were touching and then, wordlessly, we slipped into each other's arms and exchanged a huge, wet kiss. We fell back upon a small sofa and as our tongues swirled around inside the other's mouth, we each had our hand over each other's pussies, rubbing our palms against our glossy bushes.

I was particularly aroused by Sylvana's thrilling young body. She was like a sleek, pampered kitten as she arched her back in delight as I explored further between her legs and a warm, tingling feeling swept through me as the yielding lips of her cunney opened out under my gentle probes. Now I slid my hand under the firm cheeks of her delectable bum and for a short while I frigged her wrinkled little rear dimple which made her wriggle from side to side. Then I switched back to her pussey which she obviously preferred for she began to coo contentedly as I transferred my hand to her cunt, rubbing my knuckles against her sopping slit until she was breathless with excitement. I inserted one and then two fingers inside her sopping cunt and spread the lips out wide as she gurgled with delight. I rubbed harder and harder against her clitty which very soon swelled up like a little, stiff cock.

Her cuntal juices flowed like honey as I started to kiss her hard, pointed titties, licking and sucking them until they stood out like two little red bullets. I kissed her flat tummy and moved my mouth downwards to the firm curves of her pubis, slithering my lips over her dripping quim, and I tasted her tangy juices as I sucked hard on her big clitty that was projecting from between the pouting lips of her cunt, prodding it to great effect as Sylvana gasped with pleasure.

'A-h-r-e! *Magnifico, cara Rosie!*' she cried and I buried my mouth in the lavish succulent padding of pussey hair, and her love juice came gushing out as I worked my lips until my jaw ached, teasing my tongue inside the rubbery grooves of her love channel.

My hands were busy tweaking her rubbery red nipples as I placed my lips over her clitty and nibbled daintily at it before sucking up the erectile flesh into my mouth where the tip of my tongue started to explore it from all directions. Then I found the little joy button under the fold at the base of her clitty and began twirling my tongue around it. As I moved it up and down she became more and more excited and I was forced to let go of her titties and grasp her bum cheeks to maintain my oral suction. The faster I vibrated her clitty, the quicker she began to gyrate, moaning loudly and rocking her head from side to side as the juices cascaded out from between her pouting pussey lips.

Oh how wet she was! Her head was thrown back, her shoulders shaking as little quakes ran through her body whilst I lapped even quicker along the ribbed grooves of her cunney, licking up her tangy cuntal fluids which ran down like a stream and mixed with my saliva. Her pussey was now gushing love juice and each time I flicked at her clitty I felt it stiffen perceptibly, ever more eager and pulsating until with a piercing scream she exploded into a marvellous, all-embracing orgasm.

Now it was my turn to lie back, spread my legs and wait to be pleasured by Sylvana's darting tongue. She placed her pretty head against my soft blonde mount and without further ado started to lick my pussey lips which she parted with her long fingers.

She looked up at me and leaned back, her lips sticky from where she had been kissing my cunney lips and said: 'What a sweet-smelling cunt you have, Rosie. I shall give you the most exquisite licking out you have ever experienced, my dear girl.'

'I want action, not words! Finish me off with your tongue,' I pleaded and Sylvana bent forward again, her lips nuzzled against my juicy crack, teasing her tongue inside my pussey. She found my clitty and kept up a blissful rhythm of the most salacious sucking until I was so wet that I could feel my own cuntal juices dribbling down my thighs. She jabbed one, two and then three fingers inside my cunt, sliding them in and out of my pussey at breakneck speed whilst her wicked tongue lapped around my clitty.

I squeezed her head between my thighs, urging her on as I felt myself on the brink of the ultimate pleasure as waves of lust ran up and down my spine.

'Aaaah! Aaaah! You've made me come,' I panted as I spent profusely, soaking Sylvana's mouth with love juice which she greedily slurped and swallowed as I writhed from side to side into the most wonderful orgasm. However, despite the undoubted fact, as I have mentioned before in these recollections, that on the whole (please pardon the pun!) girls are far more adept at eating pussey than boys, I still prefer a thick, meaty cock in my cunt than anything else!

Be that as it may, I spent a very pleasant time with Sylvana and although I did not purchase the *robe de nuit*, I did buy a beautifully styled linen blouse and before I left, I promised to come again to Sylvana's shop for one of the exclusive fashion shows which she gave every Thursday afternoon.

I walked slowly to Otello's restaurant and looked around for young Terence. At first I thought he had not yet arrived, but then I heard him call from a table placed out on the pavement under the restaurant awning.

'Hello there, Rosie, here I am,' he cried and immediately I noticed an extraordinary change in the young man's bearing. His eyes were sparkling, his face was slightly flushed and he was possessed of a *joie de vivre* which made it plain that Father Lionel's friend had provided him with a tonic which no doctor could have prescribed!

I sat down and, after ordering a light meal of pasta and

a bottle of white wine, I prompted Terence into telling me what had happened to him inside Sophia's apartment. All must have gone well with him, for he did not demur and launched directly into an account of his visit and said: 'Oh, everything went swimmingly, Miss Rosie — and do you know, after you left me I walked up and down the Via Trippetto outside number sixty-nine for at least five minutes, very much in two minds as to whether I should keep this appointment. Luckily, I finally plucked up enough courage to ring the bell and a beautiful young blonde girl answered the door.

' "Good afternoon," I stammered hesitantly. "My name is Terence Whiter and I have an appointment with Signorina Sophia at noon."

' "Ah yes," she said in perfect English as she beckoned me inside. "Do come in, Terence, Father Lionel telephoned earlier and told me to expect you."

'I followed her into the hall and into a beautifully furnished drawing room and she asked me to sit down and make myself at home. She went on: "I'm afraid that Sophia will not be here until tonight as she is spending the day sitting for the talented American artist, Mr Jason Kelvin, who has been living in Rome since March.

' "My name is Kitty Glanville and I am also spending the summer in this wonderful city. I'm living with Sophia, who is an old friend from my days at finishing school." '

'Wait a moment, Terence,' I interrupted excitedly. 'You did say that this girl's name was Kitty Glanville?' He nodded and I clicked my fingers together and exclaimed: 'What an amazing coincidence! This shows how modern travel is making the world such a small place these days — why, I know Kitty Glanville and, come to that, her friend Sophia Visconti very well. They were both contemporaries of mine at Madame Dupont's Finishing School in Lucerne. If you are planning to see them again, you must give them my

179

kindest regards. In fact, I'll write a letter to Kitty. She is a blonde girl, petite but very pretty and hails, if I remember rightly, from Edinburgh.'

'Yes, you've described her perfectly, and she does have a very pleasant light Scottish accent,' gasped Terence. 'As well as a wonderfully generous nature, as I found out an hour or so ago.'

The waiter brought us our wine and Terence continued his story which I was now certain would have a happy ending, for whilst at Madame Dupont's establishment, both Kitty and Sophia were known as two randy girls who enjoyed nothing better than bedroom romps with Pierre, Madame Dupont's handsome young son [see 'Rosie 1: Her Intimate Diaries' — Editor]. So I listened avidly as he continued: ' "Yes, Father Lionel telephoned this morning and informed us of your problem," she said sweetly, and I must have blushed because she added hastily: "Oh, do not be ashamed, Terence. Virginity is a condition easily cured between the ages of sixteen and twenty-five. After that, it can be a little more difficult to cure."

'I smiled glassily at this remark and she returned my smile, showing pearly white teeth which sparkled in the bright, midday sunlight that poured through the large windows. Kitty was dressed in a loose white gown with short sleeves and I noticed that her feet were bare as she walked towards me. She took hold of my hand and said softly: "I was upstairs having a siesta when you called — would you like to join me?"

' "Yes please," I croaked as she took my hand and guided me upstairs into her bedroom.

'By the window of her bedroom stood an artist's easel and she said to me as she cast a critical eye over my body: "I also paint, although I doubt if I'll ever be as famous as Jason Kelvin. Would you mind modelling for me, Terence, whilst I make a quick charcoal sketch?"

' "Not in the slightest," I replied and honestly, Rosie, I had no idea what Kitty was about to suggest. "Where would you like me to stand?"

'She considered this question for a few moments and then replied: "I think you'd look best lying down on the bed."

' "Very well," I said, and took off my jacket and was about to take up a position when she said with a coy giggle: "Oh, but you'll have to take off all your clothes for me to make a proper sketch."

' "All my clothes?" I echoed, and Kitty must have sensed my modesty because she added encouragingly: "Look, if it makes you feel any easier, I'll take my clothes off, too. It's so warm today that I'll be far more comfortable working in the nude."

'Like in a dream, I sat down on a chair and took off my shoes and socks. Then I took off my trousers and my shirt, but my hands trembled as I turned around to face the wall and tugged down my drawers. "What a nice bum you have, Terence," she said with what sounded like genuine admiration in her voice. "Now turn round, there's absolutely no need for such a handsome boy like you to be shy."

'I obeyed and she told me to lie on the bed with my hands behind my head and my legs slightly apart. Then she gave me a luscious smile and ran the tip of her tongue over her top lip as she unhooked the buttons on her dress and, in one quick movement, pulled it over her head. My heart began to beat nineteen to the dozen as I looked at her beautiful body silhouetted against the light. Kitty's uptilted bare breasts bounced invitingly as she walked towards me, though I could hardly tear my eyes away from the thick fleece of blonde pussey hair at the base of her flat tummy. My cock swelled up straight away and by the time she had taken the three steps necessary to reach me, my shaft was sticking high up in the air, although my hands were still locked together behind my head. She ruffled my hair with her fingers and murmured: "Before we begin work, let's get to know each other a little more. I need to capture your very essence before I can produce anything on canvas." '

'I can imagine what essence she captured and I'll wager it didn't take very long for you to produce it,' I said roguishly, and Terence gave a little chuckle as he said: 'It didn't take very long at all. Kitty kissed me and in an instant her tongue was in my mouth, probing and rousing as my hands caressed her taut nipples, squeezing the succulent globes of her breasts whilst she clasped my pulsating prick and jerked her hand up and down my throbbing shaft. Seconds later a shuddering orgasm of pleasure ran through my body and a miniature fountain of spunk gushed out of my cock and ran down over her fingers.

' "Oh dear, we can't have you finishing before we've really begun, can we now?' she murmured and she pushed me down on the bed and began to stroke my still quivering cock with her skilful fingers. Surprisingly quickly, my shaft soon regained its former thickness and then Kitty dipped her tousled blonde head between my legs and kissed my knob. Instinctively, I heaved my hips upwards to slide my cock between her lips.

'Oh, how wonderful it was when her tongue circled my shaft and swirled around my helmet. I felt my balls hardening and shouted that I was going to come again, and so she opened her mouth and climbed on top of me with her knees on either side of my hips. She pulled open her pussey lips with her fingers and rubbed her cunney back and forth across the tip of my knob, which really drove me wild for I knew the moment of truth was finally at hand. Then, sure enough, I crossed the Rubicon as Kitty sat down on my thick prick, and somehow she managed to tighten her cunney to hold my cock in place whilst she rocked backwards and forwards upon it. She rode me hard, sliding her juicy love channel up and down my delighted prick and then she screamed out as now she began to climax. This excited me so much that I soon felt the white froth spurting upwards from my balls.

' "Yes, yes, shoot your spunk!" she yelled with joy as the hot, creamy jism flooded into her, and I pumped out my sticky seed into her dark, wet cunney as her own love juices flowed over my twitching tool. We lay there for a while, panting with exhaustion and I was in the very seventh heaven of delight, though it grieved me to think of what I had been missing!'

Terence's voice trailed off as the waiter bustled up to our table with two large bowls of *Pasta con cacio pepe*. I twirled the twists of spaghetti round my fork and said: 'May I offer my congratulations, Terence. Most people would agree that one's first fuck is a traumatic experience and I am truly delighted that your first adventure went so well. First love can be idyllic or, frankly, an absolute disaster. I hope you won't mind my saying so, but you were fortunate to be accompanied on your first journey along the highway of sensuous pleasures by an uncomplicated yet sophisticated girl who was happy to allay any fears you may have entertained about making love to her.'

Terence nodded his head vigorously. 'If truth be told, it would be more accurate to state that Kitty made love to me,' he agreed as he took a large mouthful of spaghetti. 'M'mm, this is very good, Rosie. What herbs have been mixed in with the pasta?'

'Only black pepper and cheese,' I said, and we both tucked in with relish and finished our tasty meal. 'But tell me, now, do I presume we have now come to the end of your first sexual foray?'

'Actually, no. After we had rested for a while, I was surprised to discover that my cock could still rise to the occasion when Kitty squeezed my limp shaft inside her fist.

183

"I don't think I can do any more," I whispered to her, but she winked at me and said gaily: "What, a strapping young lad like you! I'll bet you can still get a hard-on!"

'Sure enough, I soon felt the first stirrings of an erection as she slowly rubbed my stiffening shaft. Gently, she stroked the underside, allowing her fingers to trace a path around and underneath my balls which made my shaft as hard as rock, and she leaned forward and gave my knob a loving suck whilst she diddled her own pussey, slicking her finger between her sticky love lips.

' "I think you're more than ready for a final fling," she said huskily as she rolled over onto her back and motioned for me to scramble up in front of her. I was on my knees in double quick time, my knob just inches away from the gaping lips of Kitty's cunt which were pouting redly through the moist, silky hairs of her pussey bush. I brought my straining shaft and fairly ran it through the sopping depths of her juicy cunney until my ballsack swished against Kitty's bottom.

' "Lie still for a moment," she commanded, and her cuntal muscles squeezed my cock so deliciously that I almost swooned with ecstasy. Then she heaved up her bum and I responded with a mighty shove of my own and we began heaving to and fro. It crossed my mind that the waves of blissful pleasure which were coursing through my veins were those of an exciting fuck, and I knew that nothing I had ever known or would experience in the future could ever match these unique delights.

'I looked down and saw my prick working in and out of her sopping love sheath and our movements were now locked into a furious rhythm. With a choking cry Kitty panted: "Come on, Terry, give my cunt a good fucking with that luscious young cock! Faster, faster, keep thrusting! I know you have lots of lovely jism boiling in your balls!" and she clawed my back as she writhed under me with the force of

184

her approaching orgasm. We fucked at an even greater speed, until, with a tiny wail, she slumped backwards, her thighs clenched around my waist as her body shook in a rapidly drawn-out series of spasms. Her cunney squeezed my cock even more tightly and I exploded into her, shooting off a further flood of hot spunk into her saturated love channel and draining my prick so completely that it shrivelled into limpness even before I had taken it out of her love-hole.'

He sighed and closed his eyes and a slow smile creased its way across his face as he relived these marvellous, heart-stopping moments. Then as an after-thought he added: 'Of course, there was not time for Kitty to begin sketching me, but I have promised to go to her apartment tomorrow morning and she will begin work then.'

Terence's tale had stirred my own imagination, although I said nothing until we had finished our meal with some fresh fruit and coffee. I gave him some money to pay the bill and he left a lavish gratuity for the waiter, who bowed us out of the restaurant. Then we strolled back to where Carlo Nettolone's chauffeur was waiting for us – and in the car, I leaned over and whispered in his ear: 'Terence, I thoroughly enjoyed hearing the stirring story of your first fuck. Now, unless you have any objection, I want you to come back to my room here and now and let us see whether your next fuck will be just as ecstatic as your first!'

No-one appeared to be at home, except a manservant who opened the front door for us so, without further ado, we raced upstairs and once safely in my bedroom I hoisted up my skirt to take off my suspenders. Terence must also have been fired by the prospect of further erotic adventures because before I knew it the cheeky young scamp's hands had beaten mine and my suspenders were unhooked and my knickers were being pulled down.

We tumbled crazily onto the bed, tearing at each other's clothes in a lustful frenzy. I ripped open his trousers and grabbed hold of his thick, naked cock which sprang up to greet me. I delicately fingered the bulbous helmet and found out that it was already wet with jism. So, smacking my lips, I lapped up his sweet love juice whilst we continued to throw off our clothes and we were both stark naked.

Terence groaned with delight as I worked on his grand, hard cock, running my teeth gently against the ribbed nodules of his prick. Then I sucked in his ruby-mushroomed knob and swirled my tongue over the dome, washing the sensitive, uncapped crown whilst my hands fondled his heavy balls. This excited me so much that I opened my mouth and whispered fiercely: 'I must have this lovely cock inside me!' and I leaped on top of him and jammed his thick prick inside my juicy honeypot as I sat with my bare bum facing him.

Young Terence may have been inexperienced but his instincts led him firmly on the right road, for now he grasped my bum cheeks with both hands and started to squeeze them rhythmically as I pushed up and down, contracting my powerful pussey muscles with every movement so as to grip every inch of his gorgeous truncheon inside my cunt. I reached between his legs and toyed with his bollocks as I ran my fingers back along to his hairy arse and forward again to his balls, scraping the pink, wrinkled sack with my fingernails as he writhed in ecstasy underneath me.

He began to jerk his hips up and down so fast as I continued to ride him that I soon felt the tide of an approaching orgasm approach me. We moved together in perfect unison as the hard ball of his knob rubbed against my clitty and the first ripples of orgasm crackled through my veins. Flames of fire lashed through me as my clitty now throbbed with excitement, and I shrieked out loud as my cunney went into wild spasms and Terence's slim, youthful frame went rigid and his prick twitched madly before sending a torrent of warm, creamy spunk right up inside me, just as my own climax exploded into a mass of shooting stars and I ascended the highest peaks of pleasure. Our mutual emissions were so copious that my cunney overflowed with jism, and our love liquids ran down his cock and over his balls whilst we lay quivering with passion until the end of this glorious mutual spend.

Oblivious to everything but each other, we lay naked in each other's arms and fell into a light but refreshing sleep, from which we were woken by an insistent knocking on the door. I scrambled inside the covers whilst Terence leaped out of bed and slipped on his dressing gown before calling out: 'Come in.'

The door opened and the lithe figure of Fiona Robson stood framed in the doorway. 'Hello there, you lovebirds,' she drawled with a wide smile upon her attractive face. 'I am truly sorry to interrupt your canoodling, but a telegraph message has just arrived for Rosie from London.'

I sat up in bed and Fiona came up and passed the telegram to me. I dislike telegrams as I always have awful forebodings that they will contain bad news. However, in this case my fears were quite unfounded as the cable came from none other than Count Gewirtz, Terence's erstwhile host at Broadbridge Heath, where the incidents which caused Terence and Lord Philip Pelham to go into temporary voluntary exile took place.

The message read: DELIGHTED TO REPORT THAT H.M. HAS FORGIVEN AND FORGOTTEN WHAT HAPPENED AT BROADBRIDGE AND INSISTS WE ALL JOIN HIM AND MRS K IN BIARRITZ. DETAILED LETTER TO FOLLOW.

'Well, I'm glad to know that your randy old King doesn't bear grudges,' commented Fiona when I showed her the message.

187

'So am I,' chipped in Terence. 'But who the heck is Mrs K?'

Fiona and I exchanged glances and I cleared my throat and explained: 'The Count is referring to Alice Keppel. She's been the King's favourite mistress for some ten years now, and even goes to stay with him for a month or so every Easter in Biarritz.'

This little revelation shocked Terence. 'Good grief, doesn't her husband mind?' he said, and I shook my head and replied: 'He makes his own arrangements elsewhere, no doubt, and I don't believe that the Queen is too bothered by her, for Mrs Keppel is one of the few people who can deal with His Majesty's temper, which is becoming shorter by the day, as you yourself can testify.'

Fiona winked at me and said: 'Well now, Terence, I'm sure your prick is not suffering from that malady, especially since your visit to Father Lionel's friend, and now your little recreation with Rosie.'

Her hands deftly unknotted the sash of his robe and she pulled the garment off his shoulders. The handsome youth stood naked before her and Fiona weighed his heavy, semi-erect shaft in her hand and added: 'What a fine, meaty cock! Tell me, have you two been engaged in a game that only two can play, or may I join in?'

Terence didn't know how to reply, but I said cheerfully to our pretty hostess: 'Oh, I'm sure we can fit you in somehow!'

Fiona swiftly undressed and first bared her rounded white breasts, but Terence's cock swelled up and stood proudly erect when she divested herself of her knickers and exposed her luxuriant thatch of jet black pussey hair and superbly chiselled crack with its pouting red lips. She dropped to her knees and cupped his balls in her hand as she gulped his uncapped helmet into her mouth, softly biting it and tickling it with the tip of her tongue. Then she thrust the whole of the throbbing shaft between her lips and by her palating and sucking soon brought him to the brink of a spend.

Then she eased his pulsing prick from her mouth and turned her face to me and said: 'Ah, Rosie, would you diddle my pussey whilst I suck off young Terence? And then I'll get my dildo and we can play some more jolly games.'

TO BE CONTINUED

The Blue Moon Erotic Reader IV

A testimonial to the publication of quality erotica, **The Blue Moon Erotic Reader IV** presents more than twenty romantic and exciting excerpts from selections spanning a variety of periods and themes. This is a historical compilation that combines generous extracts from the finest forbidden books with the most extravagant samplings that the modern erotica imagination has created. The result is a collection that is provocative, entertaining, and perhaps even enlightening. It encompasses memorable scenes of youthful initiations into the mysteries of sex, notorious confessions, and scandalous adventures of the powerful, wealthy, and notable. From the classic erotica of **Wanton Women**, and **The Intimate Memoirs of an Edwardian Dandy** to modern tales like Michael Hemmingson's **The Rooms**, good taste, passion, and an exalted desire are abound, making for a union of sex and sensibility that is available only once in a Blue Moon.

With selections by Don Winslow, Ray Gordon, M. S. Valentine, P. N. Dedeaux, Rupert Mountjoy, Eve Howard, Lisabet Sarai, Michael Hemmingson, and many others.

The Best of the Erotic Reader

"The Erotic Reader series offers an unequaled selection of the hottest scenes drawn from the finest erotic writing." — Elle

This historical compilation contains generous extracts from the world's finest forbidden books including excerpts from **Memories of a Young Don Juan, My Secret Life, Autobiography of a** *Flea,* **The Romance of Lust,** *The Three Chums,* and many others. They are gathered together here to entertain, and perhaps even enlighten. From secret texts to the scandalous adventures of famous people, from youthful initiations into the mysteries of sex to the most notorious of all confessions, **Best of the Erotic Reader** is a stirring complement to the senses. Containing the most evocative pieces covering several eras of erotic fiction, **Best of the Erotic Reader** collects the most scintillating tales from the seven volumes of **The Erotic Reader**. This comprehensive volume is sure to include delights for any taste and guaranteed to titillate, amuse, and arouse the interests of even the most veteran erotica reader.

Order These Selected Blue Moon Titles

My Secret Life $15.95

The Altar of Venus..................... $7.95

Caning Able $7.95

The Blue Moon Erotic Reader IV $15.95

The Best of the Erotic Reader.......... $15.95

Confessions D'Amour $14.95

A Maid for All Seasons I, II $15.95

Color of Pain, Shade of Pleasure $14.95

The Governess $7.95

Claire's Uptown Girls $7.95

The Intimate Memoirs of an

Edwardian Dandy I, II, III............. $15.95

Jennifer and Nikki $7.95

Burn $7.95

Don Winslow's Victorian Erotica $14.95

The Garden of Love $14.95

The ABZ of Pain and Pleasure $7.95

"Frank" and I $7.95

Hot Sheets $7.95

Tea and Spices $7.95

Naughty Message $7.95

The Sleeping Palace.................... $7.95

Venus in Paris $7.95

The Lawyer $7.95

Tropic of Lust $7.95

Folies D'Amour $7.95

The Best of Ironwood $14.95

The Uninhibited $7.95

Disciplining Jane $7.95

66 Chapters About 33 Women $7.95

The Man of Her Dream $7.95

S-M: The Last Taboo................... $14.95

Cybersex $14.95

Depravicus $7.95

Sacred Exchange $14.95

The Rooms........................... $7.95

The Memoirs of Josephine $7.95

The Pearl $14.95

Mistress of Instruction $7.95

Neptune and Surf $7.95

House of Dreams: Aurochs & Angels ... $7.95

Dark Star $7.95

The Intimate Memoir of Dame Jenny Everleigh:

Erotic Adventures $7.95

Shadow Lane VI $7.95

Shadow Lane VII $7.95

Shadow Lane VIII $7.95

Best of Shadow Lane $14.95

The Captive I, II $14.95

The Captive III, IV, V $15.95

The Captive's Journey $7.95

Road Babe $7.95

The Story of O $7.95

The New Story of O $7.95

ORDER FORM
Attach a separate sheet for additional titles.

Title   Quantity   Price

_____   ____   _____

_____   ____   _____

_____   ____   _____

_____   ____   _____

Shipping and Handling (see charges below)   _____

Sales tax (in CA and NY)   _____

Total   _____

Name _____

Address _____

City _____ State _____ / Zip _____

Daytime telephone number _____

❏ Check   ❏ Money Order   (US dollars only. No COD orders accepted.)

Credit Card # _____ Exp. Date _____

❏ MC   ❏ VISA   ❏ AMEX

Signature _____

(if paying with a credit card you must sign this form.)

Shipping and Handling charges:*

Domestic: $4 for 1st book, $.75 each additional book. International: $5 for 1st book, $1 each additional book
*rates in effect at time of publication. Subject to Change.

Mail order to Publishers Group West, Attention: Order Dept., 1700 Fourth St., Berkeley, CA 94710, or fax to (510) 528-3444.

PLEASE ALLOW 4-6 WEEKS FOR DELIVERY. ALL ORDERS SHIP VIA 4TH CLASS MAIL.

Look for Blue Moon Books at your favorite local bookseller or from your favorite online bookseller.